"You think I need backup?"

"Everybody needs someone watching their back. Especially stubborn redheads who keep poking at mysteries no one wants to talk about." Duff circled the table. "You've officially got me."

Melanie palmed the center of his chest and kept him at arm's length. "I suppose you expect me to have your back now, too?"

"I expect you to keep being my friend." He leaned into her hand, dropping his voice to a drowsy timbre. "But make no mistake, Melanie Fiske—I will be kissing you again."

Anticipation skittered through her veins. "Friends don't kiss each other like that."

"You don't want me to kiss you again?"

Her blush betrayed her. "You know I can't hide that I like you. Maybe because you're not one of them. Or maybe because you say what you think." She snatched away the fingers that were still clinging to the firm muscles of his chest and turned a pleading gaze up to him. "Just don't lie to me, okay? I want to be able to trust you."

NECESSARY ACTION

USA TODAY Bestselling Author

JULIE MILLER

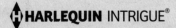

HARLEQUIN INTRIGUE®

For Tracey Marie Oberhauser.

Because you make my son happy.

Recycling programs
for this product may
not exist in your area.

ISBN-13: 978-1-335-72097-9

Necessary Action

Copyright © 2017 by Julie Miller

Printed in U.S.A.

www.Harlequin.com

Julie Miller is an award-winning *USA TODAY* bestselling author of breathtaking romantic suspense—with a National Readers' Choice Award and a Daphne du Maurier Award, among other prizes. She has also earned an *RT Book Reviews* Career Achievement Award. For a complete list of her books, monthly newsletter and more, go to juliemiller.org.

CAST OF CHARACTERS

Duff (Thomas, Jr.) Watson—This big, bad undercover cop has infiltrated a remote compound in Missouri's Ozark Mountains, looking for the source of illegal guns being smuggled into Kansas City.

Melanie Fiske—A virtual prisoner in her uncle's tiny Ozark empire. She's plain and clever and trapped in a world of misogynists and violence she desperately wants to escape.

Henry Fiske—Leader of the Fiske Family Farm. He's wealthy enough to take good care of his people. But no one escapes his family.

Abby Fiske—She'll do whatever is necessary to support her husband and ensure her daughter's happiness.

Deanna Fiske—Henry's daughter and Mel's cousin. Beautiful, but this country princess isn't as fragile or sweet as she seems.

Silas Danvers—Henry's second in command runs the farm—and several other suspicious activities.

Roy Cassmeyer—Henry Fiske's newest hire is sweet on the boss's daughter.

Daryl Renick—What secret errands is Henry sending him on?

Sue Ann Renick—Daryl's pregnant wife.

Richard Lloyd—Sue Ann's brother has been missing for four months.

Sheriff Sterling Cobb—Has Falls City elected another sheriff who's on the take?

Leroy Fiske—Melanie's late father.

Niall and Keir Watson—Duff's brothers both work for the KCPD.

Thomas Watson, Sr.—A cop himself, he knows the danger his son is facing.

Prologue

"This is some kind of Valentine's Day curse." Duff Watson stuck his finger inside the starched white collar of his shirt and tugged, certain the tux the rental shop had given him for today was a size too small.

He wondered what his family would think if he tossed the red bow tie and unbuttoned the collar of this stupid monkey suit. His sister, the bride, would be ticked, and his father would be embarrassed, Grandpa Seamus would laugh, and he'd never hear the end of it from his brothers. So he endured.

Duff—no one had called him by his given name, Tom, for years—was all for celebrating his sister's happiness. He'd even agreed to stand up as best man for her fiancé. But the only things that felt normal about Liv's wedding day were the gun holstered at the small of his back and the KCPD detective's badge stashed in his pocket. And, oh yeah, watching his two younger brothers, Niall and Keir, tagging along behind him as they escorted the bridesmaids down the aisle to join him at the altar.

The three Watson brothers, all third-generation

cops following proudly in their father's and retired grandfather's footsteps, couldn't be more different if they tried. Niall was the brain, a medical examiner with the crime lab. He seemed clueless about all the pomp and circumstance surrounding the wedding. He looked as though he was doing some sort of mental calculation about the distance to the altar or how many guests were seated in each pew. Keir was the social one, and he was eating this stuff up. He flirted with his escort and blew a kiss to the older woman in the second pew, Millie Leighter, the family cook and housekeeper who'd helped raise the four of them after their mother's senseless murder.

Duff was the self-avowed tough guy. He didn't have the multiple college degrees Niall did, and he'd never win a sweet-talking contest against Keir. But neither could match him for sheer, stubborn cussedness. Duff was the survivor. He'd been old enough when Mary Watson had died that he could see his father's anger and grief, and had stepped up to help take care of his younger siblings, even after their father had hired Millie, and Grandpa Seamus had moved in to do whatever was necessary to hold the fractured family together. Hell, even now that they were all grown-up, he was still doing whatever was necessary to protect his family—listening to his baby sister when her devil scum of a former partner had seduced and then cheated on her, making sure the man she was marrying today was worthy of her. He'd written a personal recommendation for Keir to one of his academy buddies when the ambitious youngest brother had been up for a promotion to the major crime unit. And there was no end to the coaching Niall required as the shy brainiac negotiated the intricacies of interpersonal relationships.

Duff had the street smarts, the gut instincts that helped him get through numerous undercover assignments for the department. He read people the way Niall read books. Only once had he misjudged someone he'd tried to help, and he'd paid for that mistake with his heart and a beat down that had put him in the hospital for nearly three weeks.

But facing a drug dealer's wrath hadn't killed him. Being betrayed by Shayla to her brother had only made Duff stronger and a hell of a lot smarter about falling in love. He'd been played for a fool, and he owned the repercussions of his mistake. Maybe his colossal screwup—when it came to love on this day that was all about love—was the reason he couldn't get his tuxedo to fit right.

"Natalie is married to Liv's partner, you know." Niall, an inch taller than Duff, adjusted his dark glasses and whispered the chiding remark about flirting with the bridesmaid to Keir, who stood a couple of inches shorter.

"Relax, charm-school dropout." Keir clapped Niall on the shoulder, grinning as he stepped up beside him. "Young or old, married or not—it never hurts to be friendly."

"Seriously?" Niall turned that same whispered reprimand on Duff, eyeing the middle of his back. "Are you packing today?"

He'd tucked his ankle piece into the back of his itchy wool slacks. At least he wasn't wearing his shoulder holster and Glock. "Hey. You wear your glasses every day, Poindexter. I wear my gun."

"I wasn't aware that you knew what the term 'Poindexter' meant."

"I'm smarter than I look."

Keir had the gall to laugh. "He'd have to be."

Duff shifted his stance, peering around Niall. "So help me, baby brother, if you give me any grief today, I will lay you out flat."

"Zip it. Both of you." Leave it to Niall to be the cool, calm and collected one. Liv had probably put him in charge of corralling her two rowdier brothers today. The smart guy scowled at Keir. "You, mind your manners." When Duff went after the collar hugging his neck again, Niall leaned in. "And you, stop fidgeting like a little kid."

A sharp look from the minister waiting behind them quieted all three brothers for the moment. With everything ready for their sister's walk down the aisle, the processional music started. Duff scanned the crowd as they rose to their feet. Millie dabbed at her eyes with a lace hanky, making no effort to hide her tears. He knew a hug could make those tears go away, and he would gladly go comfort her, but he was stuck up here at the altar.

Grandpa Seamus was sneaking a handkerchief out of his pocket. The old man was crying, too.

And then Olivia and their father, Thomas Watson Sr., appeared in the archway at the end of the aisle.

A few strands of gray in his dark hair, and the limp from the blown-out knee that had ended his front-line duty with the department far too soon, couldn't detract from the pride in Thomas's posture as he walked his daughter down the aisle. Duff's sinuses burned. *Be a man. Do not let your emotions get the better of you. Do not cry.*

But Olivia Mary Watson was a stunner in her long beaded gown and their mother's veil of Irish lace. Who knew that shrimp of a tomboy would grow up into such a fine, strong woman? He took after their father with his green eyes and big, stocky build. But Liv was the spitting image of the mother he remembered—dark hair, blue eyes. Walking beside Thomas Sr., he thought of the wedding picture that still sat on his father's dresser.

He blinked and had to say something quick to cover up the threat of tears. "Dude," Duff muttered. He nudged the groom beside him. "Gabe, you are one lucky son of a—"

"Duff." Niall's sharp tone reminded him that swearing in church probably wasn't a good idea.

Gabe sounded a little overcome with emotion, too. "I know."

"You'd better treat her right."

Yep. Liv must have put Niall in charge of keeping him in line today. "We've already had this conversation, Duff. I'm convinced he loves her."

Gabe never took his eyes off Olivia as he inclined his head to whisper, "He does."

Keir, of course, wasn't about to be left out of

the hushed conversation. "Anyway, Liv's made her choice. You think any one of us could change her mind? I'd be scared to try."

The minister hushed the lot of them as father and bride approached.

"Ah, hell," Duff muttered, looking up at the ceiling. So much for guarding his emotions and watching his mouth. He blinked rapidly, pinching his nose. "This is not happening to me."

"She looks the way I remember Mom," Keir said in a curiously soft voice.

Duff felt a tap on his elbow. "Do you have a handkerchief?" Niall asked.

So he'd seen the tears running down Duff's cheeks. "The rings are tied up in it."

"Here." Niall slipped his own white handkerchief to Duff, who quickly dabbed at his face. He nodded his thanks before stuffing the cotton square into his pocket and steeling his jaw against the embarrassing flare of sentiment.

When Olivia arrived at the altar, she kissed their father, catching him in a tight hug before smiling at all three brothers. Duff sniffed again, mouthing the word *beautiful* when their eyes met. Keir gave her a thumbs-up. Niall nodded approvingly. Olivia handed her bouquet off to her matron of honor and took Gabe's hand to face the minister.

The rest of the ceremony continued until the minister pronounced them husband and wife and announced, "You may now kiss the bride."

"Love you," Olivia whispered.

Gabe kissed her again. "Love you more."

"I now present Mr. and Mrs. Gabriel Knight."

Duff extended his arm to the matron of honor and followed Liv and Gabe down the aisle. He traded a wink with Grandpa Seamus, silently sharing his commiseration over the public display of emotion. He nodded to his dad and exchanged a smile with Millie before unbuttoning his jacket. The tie was going next.

He was halfway to the foyer and the freedom to unhook the strangling collar when he spied a blur of movement in the balcony at the back of the church. A figure in black emerged from the shadows beside a carved limestone buttress framing a row of organ pipes. The man opened his long duster coat, revealing the rifle and handgun he'd hidden underneath.

Duff was already pushing the matron of honor between the pews and pulling his weapon when Niall shouted, "Gun!"

The organ music stopped on a discordant note and the organist scrambled toward the opposite balcony door. The man's face was a black mask, his motives unknown. But when the stranger raised his rifle to his shoulder and took aim at the sanctuary below, his intent was crystal clear.

"Everybody down!" Duff ordered, kneeling beside the pew and raising his Beretta between his hands. "Drop it!" But the bullets rained down and he jerked back to safety.

"I'm calling SWAT," Keir shouted. Duff glanced back to see him throw an arm around Millie and pull the older woman down behind the cover of a church pew with him. Gabe Knight slammed his arms around Liv and pulled her to the marble floor beneath his body. Niall was reaching for their father and grandfather.

He heard panicked footsteps, frightened shouts and terse commands as bullets chipped away marble and splintered wood. Flower petals and eruptions of dust floated in the air. Half the guests at the wedding were cops, active duty or retired, and every man and woman was taking cover, protecting loved ones, ensuring everyone was safe from the rapid barrage of gunfire.

Duff waited for a few beats of silence before swinging out into the aisle again and crouching at the end of the pew. The gunman was on the move. So was he.

"I've got no shot," Duff yelled, pushing to his feet as the shooter dropped his spent rifle and pulled his pistol. He pointed the other officers on the guest list who happened to be armed to each exit and zigzagged down the aisle as the next hail of bullets began. "Get down and stay put!" he ordered to everyone else, and ran out the back of the sanctuary.

"Niall!" Duff heard his father shout to his brother as Duff charged up the main stairs to the second floor. By damn, if that whack job had hurt his brother, he was going down.

Signaling to another officer to cover the opposite entrance, Duff pushed open the balcony door. But he knew as soon as they entered that the balcony was clear. The chaos down below echoed through the rafters, but Duff tuned it out to focus on the staccato of running footsteps. The shooter was gone. He'd taken his weapons with him and fled through the massive church.

Duff returned to the darkened utility hallway, where a wave of cold air blew across his cheek. Outside air. Close by. The clang of metal against metal gave him direction. The perp had gone up to the roof.

His instinct was to turn to his radio and call in his location and ask for backup. But he was wearing a black tuxedo, not his uniform. He'd have to handle this himself. Leaving the other officer to see to the frightened organist, he sprinted down the hallway and climbed a narrow set of access stairs to the roof. If the perp thought he was getting out this way, he'd corner the chump before he reached one of the fire escapes.

Duff paused with his shoulder against the door leading onto the roof, reminding himself he'd be blind to the perp's position for a few seconds. Nobody shot up his sister's wedding, put his family in danger, threatened his friends. No matter what screw was loose in that shooter's head, Duff intended to stop him. Heaving a deep breath, he shoved the door open.

Squinting against the wintry blast of February air, he dove behind the nearest shelter and pressed his back against the cold metal until he could get his bearings. The glimpse of gravel and tar paper through the kicked-up piles of snow were indicators

that he wasn't the first person to come out this way.
The AC unit wasn't running, so he should be able
to hear the shooter's footsteps. Only he didn't. He
heard the biting wind whipping past, the crunch of
snow beneath tires as cars sped through the parking
lot and the muted shouts of his fellow officers, circling around the outside of the church three stories
below. The only labored breathing he could hear was
his own, coming out in white, cloudy puffs, giving
away his position like a rookie in training.

He was going to have to do this by sight. Clamp-
ing his mouth shut, he gripped his gun between his
chilling hands and darted from one cover to the next.
Instead of footprints, there was a wide trail of cleared
snow, as if the man had been dragging his long coat
behind him. But the trail was clear, and Duff followed it to the short side wall of the roof. He peered
over the edge, expecting to find a fire escape. Instead, he found a ladder anchored to the bricks that
descended to the roof of the second floor below him.
But he spotted the same odd path transforming into
a clear set of boot prints, leading across the roof to
the wall that dropped down to the parking lot.

"Got you now." Duff tucked his gun into his
pocket and slid down the ladder.

He rearmed himself as he raced across the roof.
He could make out sirens in the distance, speeding
closer. Backup from Kansas City's finest. Ambu-
lances, too. That meant somebody was hurt. That
meant a lot of somebodies in that sanctuary could
be hurt. This guy was going to pay.

Duff swung his gun over the edge of the roof and froze. "Where the hell…?"

The only thing below him was a pile of snow littered with green needles at the base of a pine tree, and another officer looking up at him, shrugging his shoulders and shaking his head.

The perp had vanished. Poof. Disappeared. Houdini must have shimmied down that evergreen tree and had a driver waiting. Either that or he was a winged monkey. How could he have gotten away?

"Son of a…" Duff rubbed his finger around the trigger guard of his Beretta before stashing it back in its holster. He was retracing his steps up the ladder, fuming under his breath, when his phone vibrated in his pocket. He pulled out his cell, saw Keir's name and answered. "He got away. The guy's a freakin' magician."

"Grandpa's been shot."

"What?" The winter chill seeped through every pore of his skin and he broke into a run. Seamus Watson, eighty-year-old patriarch, retired cop who walked with a cane, followed Chiefs football and teared up at family weddings the same way Duff did was a casualty of this mess? No. Not allowed. "How bad?"

"Bad. Niall's trying to stop the bleeding. Get down here. Now."

Duff had no one left to chase. The shooter's trail had gone as cold as the snowflakes clinging to the black wool of his tuxedo.

"On my way."

Chapter One

"Who cleans up a scuttled boat?"

Frowning at the smell of bleach filling her nose, Melanie Fiske waded barefoot into the ankle-deep water that filled the wreck of her late father's fishing boat each time it rained and opened the second aft live well, or rear storage compartment where fish and bait had once been stored. She expected to find water, rust, algae or even some sort of wildlife that had taken up residence over the past fourteen years, like the nest of slithering black water moccasins she'd found hidden inside three years ago.

Poisonous snakes had been reason enough to stop her weekly sojourn to the last place her father had been alive. But too many things had happened over the past few months in this idyllic acreage where she'd grown up—the rolling Ozark hills southeast of Kansas City—for her not to explore every available opportunity to find out what had happened to her father that night he'd allegedly drowned in the depths of Lake Hanover and was never seen again.

Now she was back, risking snakes, sunburn and the wrath of the uncle who'd raised her, to investigate the wreck, tipped over on the shoreline of Lake Hanover next to the old boat ramp that hadn't been used since the boat had been towed ashore to rot.

All these years, she'd accepted the story of a tragic accident. She'd been so young then, motherless since birth, and then fatherless, as well, that she'd never thought to question the account of that late-night fishing expedition. After an explosion in the engine, he'd fallen overboard, and the eddies near the dammed-up Wheat River power plant had dragged him down to the bottom. It had been a horrible, unfathomable tragedy.

But she'd caught her aunt and uncle in too many lies lately. She'd seen things she couldn't explain—arguments that hushed when she entered a room, trucks that arrived in the middle of the night to take handcrafts or baked goods to Kansas City, fishing excursions where no one caught a thing from the well-stocked lake. And maybe most importantly, her uncle's control was tightening like a noose around her life. There were rules for living on the farm now that hadn't been there when she'd been a teenager, and consequences for breaking them that bordered on abuse.

Yes, there were bound to be flaring tempers as they transitioned from a simple working farm to a stopping place for tourists from the city seeking outdoor fun at the lake's recreational area or a simple taste of country life without driving farther south to Branson and Table Rock Lake. There were reasons to celebrate, too. The farm had grown from a few family members running a mom-and-pop business to a small community with enough people living on the 500-acre property to be listed as an unincorporated township. But Uncle Henry still ran it as though they were all part of the same family. Their homes and small businesses were grouped like a suburban neighborhood nestled among the trees and hills. Instead of any warm, fuzzy sense of security, though, Melanie felt trapped. There were secrets lurking behind the hardworking facades of the family and friends who lived on the Fiske Family Farm.

Secrets could hurt her. Secrets could be dangerous.

When she'd hiked out to the cove to look for fourteen-year-old bloodstains or evidence of a heroic struggle to stay afloat after the engine had blown a softball-sized hole in the hull of the boat, Melanie hadn't expected to find new waterproof seals beneath the tattered seat cushions that closed off the storage wells. The first fiberglass live well she'd checked had been wiped clean. Blessedly free of snakes, this second storage compartment also smelled like bleach.

Only this one wasn't completely empty.

Curiosity had always been a trait of hers. Her father had encouraged her to read and explore and ask questions. But her uncle didn't seem to share the same reverence for learning. The last time she'd been caught poking around for answers up in her uncle's attic, she'd been accused of stirring up painful memories of a lost brother, and not being grateful for the sacrifices her aunt Abby and uncle Henry had made, taking in an eleven-year-old orphan and raising her alongside their own daughter. Melanie had moved out of the main house that very night and things had been strained between them ever since. And though she wasn't sure how much was her imagination and how much was real, Melanie got the sense that she had more eyes on her now than any bookish, plain-Jane country girl like her ever had.

Squinting into the thick forest of pines and pin oaks and out to the glare of the waves that glistened like sequins on the surface of the wind-tossed lake, Melanie ensured she was alone before she twisted her long auburn hair into a tail and stuffed it inside the back of her shirt. Then she knelt beside the opening and stuck her arm inside the tilted boat's storage well. The water soaking into the knees of her blue jeans was warm as she stretched to retrieve the round metal object. Her fingers touched cold steel and she slipped one tip inside the ring to hook it onto her finger and pull it out.

But seeing the black ring out in the sunlight didn't solve the mystery for her. Melanie closed the live well and sat on the broken-down cushion to study the object on her index finger. About the circumference of a quarter and shaped like a thick washer with a tiny protrusion off one edge, the round piece of steel had some surprising weight to it. Unravaged by nature and the passage of time, the ring couldn't be part of the original shipwreck. But what was it and how had it gotten there?

With a frustrated sigh, she shoved the black steel ring into her jeans. Her fingers brushed against a softer piece of metal inside her pocket and she smiled. Melanie jumped down onto the hard-packed ground that had once been a sandy beach and tugged the second object from her pocket as she retrieved her boots and socks.

It was her father's gold pocket watch. She traced her finger around the cursive *E* and *L* that had been engraved into the casing. A gift from her mother, Edwina, to her father, Leroy Fiske had never been without it. From the time she was a toddler, Melanie could remember seeing the shiny gold chain hooked to a belt loop on his jeans, and the prized watch he'd take out in the evenings to share with his daughter.

But the happy memory quickly clouded with suspicion. The workings of the watch had rusted with time, and the small photograph of her mother inside had been reduced to a smudge of ink. Melanie closed the watch inside her fist and fumed. If her father's body had never been found, and he always had the watch with him, then how had it shown up, hidden away in a box of Christmas ornaments in her uncle's attic?

Had this watch been recovered from the boat that fateful night? Why wouldn't Leroy Fiske have been wearing it? Had it gone into the lake with him? Who would save the watch, but not the man?

The whine of several small engines dragged Melanie from her thoughts.

Company. She dropped down behind the boat to hide. Someone had borrowed two or three of the farm's all-terrain vehicles and was winding along the main gravel road through the trees around the lake. Maybe it was one of the resident fishing guides, leading a group of tourists to the big aluminum fishing dock past the next bend of the lake, about a mile from her location. It could be her cousin Deanna, taking advantage of her position as the resident princess by stealing away from her job at the farm's bakery and going out joyriding with one of the young farmhands working on the property this summer.

"Mel?" A man's voice boomed over the roar of the engines. "You out here? Mel Fiske, you hear me?"

"Great," she muttered. It was option C. The riders were out looking for her. As the farm's resident EMT-paramedic, she knew there could be a legitimate medical reason for the men to be searching for her. Minor accidents were fairly common with farm work. And some folks neglected their water intake and tried to do too much, easily overheating in Missouri's summer heat. But she really didn't want to be discovered. Not here at her father's boat. Not when her aunt had asked her to leave the past alone, since stirring up memories of Henry's brother's drowning upset her uncle when he needed to be focusing on

important business matters. Finding her here would
certainly upset someone.

Like a swarm of bees buzzing toward a fragrant
bed of flowers, the ATVs were making their way down
through the trees, coming closer. Melanie glanced up
at the crystal blue sky and realized the sun had shifted
to the west. She'd been gone for more than two hours.
No wonder Henry had sent his number-one guard dog
to search for her.

It wasn't as if she could outrun a motorized four-
wheeler. She glanced around at the dirt and rocks
leading down to the shoulder-high reeds and grasses
growing along the shoreline. She couldn't outswim
the men searching for her, either. Her gaze landed on
the sun-bleached wood dock jutting into the water
several feet beyond the reeds. Or could she?

Melanie unzipped her jeans and crawled out of
them. After tucking the watch safely inside the
pocket with the mysterious steel ring, she stripped
down to her white cotton panties and support bra and
sprang to her feet. With a little bit of acting and a
whole lot of bravado, she raced onto the listing dock
and dove into the lake.

The surface water was warm with the summer's
blistering heat, but she purposely swam down to the
murky haze of deeper water to cool her skin and soak
her hair so that it would seem she'd been out in the
water for some time, oblivious to ATVs, shouting
voices and family who wanted her to account for
all her time.

She didn't have to outswim anybody. She just had

to make up a good cover story to explain why she'd gone for a dip in her underwear instead of her sensible one-piece suit. Melanie was several yards out by the time she kicked to the surface.

As she'd suspected, she saw two men idling their ATVs on the shore near the footing of the dock. The bigger man, the farm's foreman and security chief, who thought shaving his head hid his receding hairline, glared at her with dark eyes. He waved aside the other man, telling him to move on. "Radio in that she's okay. Then get on over to the fishing dock to make sure it's ready for that group from Chicago tomorrow."

The other man nodded. He pulled the walkie-talkie from his belt and called into the main house to report, "We found her, boss," before revving the engine and riding away. Meanwhile, Melanie pushed her heavy wet hair off her face and began a leisurely breast stroke to the end of the dock.

Silas Danvers watched her approach. "What are you doing out here?"

It wasn't a friendly question. As usual, Silas was on edge about something or someone. But, then, when wasn't the short-tempered brute ticked off about something?

Melanie opted for a bimbo-esque response he seemed to find so attractive in her cousin. She treaded water at the edge of the dock, even though she could probably stretch up on her tiptoes and stand with her head above the water. "It's a hundred degrees out here. What do you think I'm doing?"

She was getting good at lying. Maybe it was a family trait she'd inherited from her uncle.

"Why can't you just take a bath like a normal woman? Get your ass out of the water," he ordered. "You're out of cell range here."

Melanie stopped moving and curled her toes into the mud beneath her, feeling a twinge of guilt. "Is there an emergency?"

"No, but Daryl's been trying to get a hold of you. He's got a question about those medical supplies you asked him to pick up in town. No sense him making two trips just because you decided to go skinny-dipping."

Melanie nodded and paddled to the tarnished copper ladder at the edge of the dock. "Okay. I'll get out as soon as you leave."

"You got nothin' I ain't seen before." Well, he hadn't seen hers, and she wasn't about to show him. Still, she had a feeling that Silas's reluctance to turn the ATV around and ride away had less to do with her being nearly naked and more to do with his egoistic need to make sure his orders were followed. "Don't keep Daryl waiting."

Melanie held on to the ladder until he had gunned the engine and disappeared through the line of trees at the top of the hill. *Victory.* Albeit a small one. Once his shiny bald head had vanished over the rise, Melanie wasted no time climbing out of the water and hurrying back to her pile of clothes and newly acquired treasure. She was dressed from T-shirt to toes and wringing out her hair in a matter of minutes. Despite the humidity, the air was hot enough that her clothes would dry off soon enough, although her hair would kink up into the kind of snarling mess that only Raggedy Ann fans could appreciate. Funny how she'd grown up without being noticed—she'd always been a little too plump, a little too freckled, a little too into her books to turn heads. Now she was counting on that same anonymity to allow her to return to the farm without drawing any more attention to herself.

Pulling her phone from her lace-up work boot, she verified that she was, indeed, far enough out in the hills, away from the cell tower on the farm, that she had no service. So Silas hadn't lied about his reason for tracking her down. She'd give Daryl a call as soon as she was in range, and then, even though an internet connection was spottier than cell reception in this part of the state, she'd try to get online and research some images to see if she could identify the object she'd found inside her father's boat.

Putting off her amateur sleuthing for the time being, Melanie cut across to one of the many paths she and her father had explored when he'd been alive. She followed a dry creek bed around the base of the next hill and climbed toward the county road that bordered the north edge of the property.

As she'd hoped, she was able to get cell reception there, and she contacted her friend Daryl to go over the list of items she needed to restock her medical supplies. But it was taking so long to connect to the internet that she reached the main homestead and had to slip her phone into her hip pocket so that no one would see her trying to contact the outside world.

As the trees gave way to land cleared for farming, buildings, gravel roads and a parking lot, Melanie headed to the two-bedroom cottage she called home. But, instead of finding everyone going about their work for the day, she saw that a crowd had gathered near the front porch of her uncle's two-story white house. She could hear the tones of an argument, although she couldn't make out the words. Suddenly the crowd oohed and gasped as if cheering a hit in a softball game, and Melanie stopped. "What the heck?"

She changed course and headed to the main house, looking for a gap where she could get a clear view of whatever they were watching.

She spotted Silas near the bottom of the porch steps, slowly circling to his left, eyeing his unlucky target. What a surprise, discovering him in the vicinity of angry words. It was a fight, another stupid fight because somebody had ticked off Silas. More than likely, her cousin had turned him down for another date, and his opponent was merely the outlet for his wrath. Typically, her uncle didn't allow the tourists visiting the bakery and craft shop to see any kind of dissension in the ranks of the people who lived and worked on the farm. But the hot day made it easy for tempers to rile, so maybe Henry was letting one of the hands or Silas himself blow off a little steam.

Shaking her head at the testosterone simmering in the air, Melanie turned to leave behind what was sure to be a short brawl. If it even came to fists. The men around here were smart enough to end any argument with Silas with words and walk away before it escalated into something they'd regret. If these folks had gathered for some kind of boxing match, they were going to be disappointed.

Melanie halted in her tracks when Silas's opponent shifted into view.

He was new.

Her stomach tied itself into a knot of apprehension as she took in the unfortunate soul who'd been foolish enough to stand up to the farm foreman. Only it was pretty hard to think of the narrow-eyed stranger mirroring Silas's movements step for step as any kind of *unfortunate*.

The stranger was almost as tall as Silas. The faded army logo T-shirt he wore fit like a second skin over shoulders and biceps that were well muscled and broadly built. With military-short hair and beard stubble the color of tree bark shading his square jaw, he certainly looked tough enough to take on the resident bully, and she felt herself wanting to cheer for him. She caught a glimpse of a navy blue bandanna in his back jeans pocket, and her gaze lingered there long enough to realize she was gawking like a hungry woman eyeing a new batch of cupcakes in the bakery window.

Feeling suddenly warmer than the summer weather could account for, she forced herself to move away from the circle. She didn't want to watch a fight and she didn't want to be interested in any man who'd shown up here, especially since her goal was to find out about her father and then get away from this pastoral prison.

"This is how you welcome somebody to your place, Fiske?"

Melanie stopped at the stranger's deep, growly voice. *Welcome?* The apprehension left her stomach and siphoned into her veins. But she wasn't feeling pity over a pending beat down—this trepidation was all about her. If Henry had hired this guy to work on the farm, then he'd be one more Silas-sized obstacle she'd have to outmaneuver in order to keep digging for answers about her father.

Chapter Two

Duff spit the blood from his mouth where the bruiser with the shaved head had punched him in the jaw, scraping the inside of his cheek across his teeth. He eyed the older man who'd invited him here for this so-called interview standing up on the porch watching the scuffle in the grass with a look of indifference. "Forget it. I don't need a job that badly."

He wanted to get hired on at the Fiske Family Farm. If this undercover op was going to be a success, he *needed* to get hired here. But he couldn't seem too eager, too willing to kowtow to the owner's authority or to the bruiser with the iron fist's intimidation tactics. Otherwise, nobody here in the crowd of farmhands, shopkeepers and tourists—along with a man in a khaki uniform shirt sipping coffee and noshing on a Danish—would buy his big-badass-mercenary-for-hire persona. He'd spent the past few weeks cultivating his world-weary Duff Maynard identity in the nearby town of Falls City. Portraying a messed-up former soldier looking for a job off the grid, he'd even slept several nights in his truck, solidifying his lone-drifter status so that he could infiltrate the suspected illegal arms business being run behind the bucolic tranquility of this tree-lined farming and tourist commune. Playing his part convincingly was vital to any undercover op.

So he scooped up the army-issue duffel bag that had been taken from him and strode over to the porch, where Baldy had retreated to stand in front of his boss, Henry Fiske. Duff nodded toward the keys, wallet, gun and sheathed hunting knife lying on the gray planks, where the man with the shaved head sat in front of the railing, panting through his smug grin. Removing the weapons from his bag and identification from his pockets when the big man had patted him down and gone through his things had given Duff reason to start the fight in the first place, solidifying his tough-guy character in front of a lot of witnesses. "I'll be taking those."

Baldy rose to his feet, looking ready, willing and eager to go another round with him. "I don't think so, Sergeant Loser," he taunted.

He heard a few worried whispers moving through the onlookers as he and Baldy faced off. But the man on the porch, Henry Fiske, raised his hand and quieted them. "Not to worry, folks. We're just gettin' acquainted. Had a bit of a misunderstanding that we'll work out." He gestured to the uniformed man standing near the end of the porch. "Besides, we've got Sheriff Cobb here. So nothing bad's gonna happen. Go back to your cars or get to shoppin'." He tipped his nose and sniffed the air. "I smell fresh baked goods y'all aren't going to want to miss."

With murmurs of approval and relief, most of the touristy types separated from the crowd and headed toward the shops on the property. But others—the men and women who lived and worked on the vast complex, perhaps—merely tightened their circle around Duff and the front of the house. Why weren't they dispersing as ordered? What did they know that Duff didn't?

"You've got everything under control, Henry?" the sheriff asked.

"I do."

"Then I'll be headin' back into town." He gently elbowed the sturdy, fiftysomething blonde woman beside him. "I just drove out to get some of Phyllis's tasty cooking. My wife doesn't fix anything like this for dessert."

The woman waved off the compliment and turned to follow the tourists. "Come on, Sterling. I'll pack a box of goodies to take with you."

That's why the Hanover County sheriff hadn't been included in the task force working this case. Either Sterling Cobb was being paid to overlook any transgressions here, or the portly man who'd refused to step in and break up a fight was afraid, incompetent or both.

"Ain't nobody here to back you up, Sergeant Loser," Baldy taunted as soon as the sheriff was out of earshot. "You still want to give me trouble?"

In real life, Duff had been an officer, not a noncom, and he bristled at the dig. But he was playing a part here on behalf of KCPD and the joint task force he was working for. His fake dossier said he'd enlisted out of high school and had seen heavy action in the Middle East, which had left him disillusioned, antisocial and a perfect fit for the homegrown mafia allegedly running arms into Kansas City.

Like the guns that had been used to shoot up his sister's wedding and put his grandfather in the hospital.

Duff had to play this just right. Because he was not leaving until he had not only the job, but the trust—or at least the respect—of the people here so that he could work his way into Fiske's inner circle. He'd need that freedom of movement around the place to gather the intel that could put Fiske and the operation he was running out of business.

Although his mission briefing for this joint task force undercover op between KCPD, the Missouri Bureau of Investigation and the ATF hadn't mentioned any welcome-to-the-family beat down, Duff had worked undercover enough that he knew how to think on his feet. He'd originally thought this assignment had more to do with his familiarity with the terrain of the Ozark Mountains, where he'd spent several summers camping, hunting and fishing. But he also knew how to handle himself in a fight. And if that's what the job called for, he'd milk his tough-guy act for all it was worth.

He stepped into Baldy's personal space and picked up the Glock 9mm in its shoulder holster, stuffing both it and the knife inside his duffel bag. He kept his gaze focused on Baldy's dark eyes as he retrieved the ring of keys and wallet with his false IDs and meager cash. Interesting. Baldy's jaw twitched as though he wanted to resume the fight, but the man standing above them on the porch seemed to have his enforcer on a short leash.

"In town you told me I had a job here at the farm if I wanted it." He shifted his stance as Baldy spit at that promise and pushed to his feet. There had to be somebody here he could make friends with to get the inside scoop. Clearly, it wasn't going to be Baldy. "Tell him to back off. You said you needed a man who knew something about security. I didn't realize you offered blood sport as one of your tourist attractions."

"I believe you were the one to throw the first punch, Mr. Maynard." Fiske gestured to the people waiting for the outcome of this confrontation. "We all saw it. Silas was defending himself."

Henry Fiske might have looked unremarkable in any other setting. He was somewhere in his fifties, with silvering sideburns growing down to his jaw and into his temples. He wore overalls and a wide-brimmed straw hat that marked him as a man who worked the land. The guy even had an indulgent smile for the platinum blonde leaning against the post beside him. The aging rodeo queen would be his wife, Abby. Despite Fiske's friendly drawl, Duff had seen the cold expectation that his authority would not be challenged in eyes like Fiske's before.

So, naturally, Duff challenged it. He swung his duffel bag onto his shoulder. "I'm out of here."

"Don't let the muck on my boots fool you, Mr. Maynard. I'm a businessman." Duff kept walking. "A lot of money and traffic pass through here in the summertime, making us a target for thieves and vandals. Hanover is a big county for the sheriff to patrol, and since we're a remote location, we're often forced to be self-sufficient. It's my responsibility to see the property and people here stay safe." A mother pulled a curious toddler out of the way and the crowd parted to let him pass toward the gravel parking lot in front of the metal buildings where he'd parked his truck. "I needed to see if your skills are as good as you claim. You don't exactly come with reputable references."

"The US Army isn't a good enough reference for you?" Duff halted and turned, reminding Fiske of the forged document that was part of the identification packet the task force had put together for him to establish his undercover identity—Sergeant Thomas "Duff" Maynard. His army service was real, but the medical discharge and resulting mental issues that made him a bad fit for "normal" society had been beefed up as part of his undercover profile.

"I trust what I see with my own eyes. Silas?" Henry Fiske called the big man back into action and gave a sharp nod in a different direction.

The crowd shifted again as a second man approached from the right. This twentysomething guy was as lanky as Silas was overbuilt. But the scar on his sunburned cheek indicated he knew his way around a brawl. So this was what the crowd had been waiting for—a two-on-one grudge match. This wasn't any different than a gang initiation in the city. If Fiske wanted Duff to prove he had hand-to-hand combat skills, then prove it he would.

Duff pulled the duffel bag from his shoulder and swung it hard as Skinny Guy charged him. The heavy bag caught the younger man square in the gut and doubled him over. He swung again, smashing the kid in the face before dropping the bag and bracing for Baldy's attack. The big man named Silas grabbed Duff from behind, pinning his arms to his sides. He hoped Baldy had a good grip on him because he used him as a backboard to brace himself and kick out when Skinny Guy rushed him a second time. His boot connected with the other man's chin and snapped his head back, knocking him on his butt. Utilizing his downward momentum, Duff planted his feet and twisted, throwing Baldy off his back.

But the big guy wasn't without skills. He hooked his boots around Duff's legs and rolled, pulling him off balance. The grass softened the jolt to Duff's body, but the position left him vulnerable to the kick to his flank that knocked him over.

Baldy was on him in a second and they rolled into the wood steps at the base of the porch, striking the same spot on his ribs. Duff grimaced at the pain radiating through his middle, giving his attacker the chance to pop him in the cheek and make his eyes water. Okay. Now he was mad. Time to get real.

He slammed his fist into Baldy's jaw and reversed their positions. Duff pinned his forearm against the big man's throat, cutting off his air supply until his struggles eased, and he slapped the bottom step as if the gesture was his version of saying *Uncle*.

Silas might be done with the fight, but by the time Duff had staggered to his feet, Skinny Guy had, too.

"Stay down!" Duff warned. But when he swung at him, anyway, Duff dropped his shoulder and rammed the other man's midsection, knocking the younger guy's breath from his lungs and laying him flat on the ground.

Duff was a little winded himself, and damn, he was going to be sore tomorrow. But as far as he could tell from the cheering hoots from a couple of teenage boys, he'd passed this part of the job interview with flying colors. He was brushing bits of grass and dirt from the thighs of his jeans and checking the dribble of blood at the corner of his mouth when the cheers abruptly stopped.

He heard a grunt of pure, mindless fury behind him and spun around. He saw the glint of silver in Baldy's hand a split second before a slash of pain burned through the meat of his shoulder. Duff dodged the backswing of the knife, and jumped back another step when the blade was shoved toward his belly.

He was poised to grab Baldy's wrist on the next jab when a blur of warm auburn hair and faded blue jeans darted into the space between them. "Stop! Silas, stop!"

Instinctively, Duff snaked his uninjured arm around the woman's waist and pulled her away from the thrusting knife. "Are you crazy?"

Baldy, too, seemed shocked by the interloper. He grabbed the redhead by the wrist and jerked her from Duff's one-armed grasp before pushing her to the side. "Damn it, girl. You get out of my way."

She stumbled a few feet. But as soon as she found her footing, the redhead jumped right back into the fray. She shoved at Silas's chest and wedged herself between the two men. "I said to stop!"

Duff's arm went around her again, snugging her round bottom against his hip as he spun her away from the danger and pulled her to a safer distance. "Listen, sweetheart, I appreciate the effort, but you're going to get yourself killed. And I can't have that on my con—"

"Melanie!" Henry Fiske shouted from the porch, warning the woman to stand down instead of telling Baldy to lower the knife that was now pointed at both of them. "You forget yourself, girl. You get out of there now. This doesn't concern you."

Silas's dark gaze bored into hers and Duff retreated another step, dragging his foolhardy savior farther from that blood-tipped blade. Silas snapped his gaze up to Duff's, over the top of her head, before he flicked the knife down into the ground and walked over to the edge of the porch. Cursing Duff and the woman under his breath, Baldy dipped his hands into a bucket of water and splashed it over the top of his dirty, sweaty head.

A damp wisp of wavy auburn hair lifted in the hot summer breeze and stuck to the sweat on Duff's neck as his chest heaved against the exertion of the fight. The woman's breath was coming hard, too, but she kept her eyes fixed on Silas, making sure he wasn't going to try another sneak attack. She sagged against Duff's chest, and he realized the front of his khaki T-shirt was soaking up moisture from the long cords of hair caught between them. As quickly as he sensed the woman's relief, he realized he was still holding on to her with a death grip. He released her and she turned to inspect the torn, bloodied cotton of his sleeve. Well, hell. She might be a lot of tough talk, but she was gutting her way through this brave little rebellion against his violent welcome.

"I'm forgetting nothing, Uncle Henry. The new guy put Silas down fair and square. He proved what you wanted him to." Despite her succinct words, there was a soft drawl to her *ng*'s and vowel sounds, indicating her Ozark upbringing. "You put me in charge of the infirmary and I'm doing my job. I know you sent Daryl on a supply run, but until we restock, I don't have the supplies to treat more injuries like this."

She reminded him of a long-haired Irish setter after a bath, with the dripping ends of her long hair making dark spots on the front of her gray T-shirt. She was of average height and definitely on the full-figured side of things. Her face was nothing remarkable to look at. Ordinary brown eyes. Simple nose and apple-shaped cheeks dusted with freckles. Pale pink lips.

But her fingers worked with beautiful precision. She ripped the sleeve away and pulled the material down off the end of his arm before wadding it up and pressing it against the slice across the outside of his shoulder. She didn't even hesitate at his grunt of pain. The woman certainly knew how to make a field dressing. "As it is, I may not have enough sutures to seal this cut. And I'm completely out of antibiotics. We should take him to the hospital in Falls City."

"Is he dying?" Fiske asked.

The redhead's mouth squeezed into a frown. "No."

"Then you're not going anywhere. You're a resourceful girl. Figure it out." Fiske's tone made that sound more like an annoyance than the compliment it should have been. And there was nothing girlish about the curves straining the damp T-shirt she wore. "Have you been in the lake again, Mel?"

"I took a dip to cool off." That explained the wet hair.

"Melanie?" Fiske chided, apparently requiring a different sort of answer.

She dropped one hand from the makeshift dressing over Duff's shoulder and lowered her head to a more deferential posture. "I'll find a way to take care of him without going to town."

Without the pressure of her grip, the cut throbbed and blood trickled down his arm again. Thinking she'd given up on defying her uncle to help him, Duff snagged the wadded cotton from her grip and reached over to cover the wound with his own hand. But she surprised him by stretching around him and palming his backside. Her heavy breasts squished against his chest as she patted one cheek and then the other. The grope was unexpected but far more pleasurable than Silas's fist had been. Duff turned to keep her eyes in sight, gauging her intent. "Not that I don't appreciate a good butt-grab, sweetheart, but I don't even know your last name."

"It's Fiske…oh." Rosy dots appeared beneath her freckles as her gaze darted up to his. Her fingers stroked him as she curled them into her palm, and his buttock muscle clenched at the unintended tickle. She pulled back, dangling the blue bandanna she'd stolen from his pocket. "Um…"

"You stopped that girl's mouth from runnin', Mr. Maynard." Fiske chuckled from the porch. "You're hired."

Chapter Three

"Mr. Maynard."

With his brain sidetracked by the blush creeping up Melanie's neck, Duff didn't immediately answer to the name on his fake driver's license. She not only hadn't been getting fresh with him, but she looked mortified for him to believe that she had been. Duff backed away a step, silently cursing how easily her bold touches had distracted him. And this feisty mouse wasn't even trying! *Reel it in, Watson.* She was being resourceful, just as her uncle had directed, not putting the moves on him.

He knew better than to let any woman get in his head and derail his focus on his assignment. He looked over the top of Melanie's wild red hair and nodded his thanks to her uncle. "I trust the open space and quiet time to think you promised me starts now?" He glanced around the circle of lingering onlookers and hardened his voice to a steely timbre. "Or does anybody else want to try to get their licks in?"

Fiske laughed as a few less-daring souls skittered away from the audience. "I promise we have a predictable routine and plenty of opportunities for you to make a living away from outside influences here." The laughter ended as Henry eyed the slender young woman who had hurried over to help Skinny Guy off the ground. No doubt suffering from battered pride in addition to his bloody nose, he seemed only too happy to drape his arm around the pretty brunette's shoulders and limp toward the side of the house. "Roy?" Skinny Guy turned. "You did well today. You didn't quit. I can't ask for anything more."

Roy nodded. "Yes, sir. Thank you, sir."

"But you aren't going anywhere alone with my daughter," he warned. "Silas, you take Deanna on into the house."

"Yes, sir." The big guy seemed eager to obey that order.

"Silas will do nothing of the kind." The blonde who'd been leaning against the post walked to the edge of the porch to rest her hand on her husband's arm. "Young people need a little time to themselves."

Henry patted his wife's hand before seeking out his daughter. "All right, then, tend to Roy. But, remember, dinner's at six, and I expect to see you there. We have company coming."

"Who? Silas?" the young brunette whined. "He's not company."

"You do as I say, young lady," Henry ordered.

"Daddy—"

"Deanna Christine…"

The young brunette looked from her mother to her father. "What if Roy and I have plans? I'm not a baby, anymore. I'm almost twenty-two. You can't tell me what to do."

"Six o'clock, young lady. Or you won't be seeing Roy at all."

Deanna pouted out her copper-tinted lips. "Yes, Daddy." She wound her arm around Roy's waist and leaned into him. "Come on. I'll make those boo-boos feel all better."

Abby squeezed her husband's arm before retreating to the corner of the porch to watch her daughter leave. "She'll be fine, dear. I promise."

Leaving his daughter's love life up to his wife's supervision, Henry repeated his order. "Give Mr. Maynard his bag and get cleaned up."

Silas waited for a moment, then pulled the knife that was stained with Duff's blood out of the ground. He held the blade down at his side as he picked up the duffel bag. Since Melanie was working on a field dressing for his cut again, Duff reached out to take the bag. "Thanks, Baldy."

The big man didn't immediately release the strap. His eyes sent the message that he was top dog at this place. "You may have the job, but you're still on probation, Maynard. And you'll be reporting to me."

Duff was a big man, too. And backing down wasn't part of the role he needed to play. He yanked the bag from Silas's grip. "Just don't expect me to salute you."

Silas's nostrils flared. He muttered something under his breath before wrapping his big bear paw around Melanie's elbow and pulling her away from her work. "You're going to that dance with me in a couple of weeks."

It wasn't a question. Despite Duff's vow to keep his hormones in check on this assignment, he dropped the bag to pry Silas's hand off the woman.

"Are you kidding?" But the curvy redhead didn't need his help. She smacked Silas's hand away and gestured toward the corner of the house where the young couple had turned out of sight. "Ask Deanna if she's who you want to be with. I'm not interested in being her substitute."

"Silas." The vein throbbing in the big man's forehead receded at Henry's summons. "Now's not the time to be thinking about who you're taking to the Hanover Lake festival. On second thought, you clean up later. We have work lined up that needs to be dealt with today. There's a truck coming in later tonight."

"Yes, sir."

"Wipe your feet," Abby reminded the two men as they entered the main house. "And take your hat off, Henry. Don't worry, dear. I'll keep an eye on Deanna."

The two men disappeared into a room on the left side of the hallway before the front door closed. Fiske's office? Definitely a place Duff wanted to get a firsthand look at. And he wanted eyes on that truck, to see whatever was being shipped in or out. But it was too soon to make a move without raising suspicions. Fiske and his lieutenant were probably discussing him and where they could put him to work. Hopefully, something on a night shift so that there'd be fewer people to see his comings and goings when he left the compound to meet with his task-force handler.

"Welcome to our farm, Mr. Maynard." Abby Fiske offered him a silky smile as she came down the stairs. She swung her long hair off her shoulders and glanced at the redhead. "You couldn't spare a minute to put on a little makeup, dear?" she chided before giving him a head-to-toe once-over that made him feel like some kind of prize bull that was up for sale. "My husband will send someone for you when he's ready. Now all of you—the show's over." She shooed the remaining onlookers back to their jobs before she, too, disappeared around the corner of the house.

Once Duff confirmed the key players and uncovered how the illegal operation worked, he'd be one step closer to finding the man who'd pulled the trigger that had left Seamus Watson with a traumatic brain injury and a long road to recovery. Grandpa Seamus had learned to walk again, and was regaining some use of his left hand. But retraining himself to speak and enduring months of painful physical therapy had left the once-vibrant octogenarian a white-haired shell of his former self.

No one else had been shot at Liv's wedding. Only Seamus. That afternoon in February had been all about creating terror, about destroying his family's happiness and leaving them in a state of guarded vigilance in the months that followed. Somebody had to pay for that. Although his brother Niall had

saved their grandfather's life and uncovered the type
of weapons used in the shooting, and Keir had gotten
them a lead on the shooter himself, the KCPD de-
tectives officially working the case hadn't gotten the
shooter's name. All indications were that the shooter
was a hired gun going by the code name *Gin Rickey*
and that the weapons he'd used could be traced to this
backwoods retreat—the Fiske Family Farm.

Maybe everyone here was part of the arms-
smuggling ring, including the sheriff. Or maybe
most of these people were innocent, unaware of the
crimes being committed right under their noses.
And maybe they knew, but were too cowed by Fiske
and the tag team of Silas and Roy to do anything but
look the other way. No matter what, Duff intended
to get the evidence he needed to report back to his
task-force contact the next time he—

"Ow." Duff's shoulder throbbed as Melanie Fiske
pinched the bandanna around his deltoid. Right.
There was one other player in the mix here—Fiske's
niece, Melanie. Out of every person here—man or
woman—she'd been the only one to stand up to Silas
and her uncle. Maybe she was part of the smuggling
ring, too, and had stepped in before they wound up
with a dead body to dispose of. Or maybe she just
had the brassy temperament to match her red hair.
"Easy, sweetheart. I've only got two arms."

"How's your tetanus shot?" she asked, tying off
the short ends into a square knot.

His red-haired rescuer picked up the heavy duffel bag before he could grab it and hefted it onto her

shoulder. "Your bedside manner needs a little work. You sure you've got training for this?"

"I'm a registered EMT-paramedic. Uncle Henry's goal is to make the farm a completely self-sufficient community. I'm what passes for health care here." She crossed the yard, heading toward the row of cabins and bungalows on the other side of the gravel road that ran in front of the Fiskes' house. "Come with me. I need to stitch up your arm. You could use an ice pack on that cheekbone, too."

"Yes, ma'am."

She halted and spun around. "I don't appreciate being mocked. You can call me Mel or Melanie or Miss Fiske. Save the *ma'am* for my aunt Abby, and the *sweethearts* and jokes for one of the other girls if you want to impress somebody." With that bossy pronouncement, she turned and headed out again.

His gaze dropped shamelessly to the butt bobbing beneath his duffel bag as he fell into step behind her. She might dress and talk like a tomboy, but there was nothing but shapely woman filling out those jeans. Not that her curves made any difference to his assignment, but he wouldn't be much of a man if he couldn't appreciate the scenery around this place.

"Okay, Mel. I'm Tom. Tom Maynard." Using his real first name and an old family name was supposed to make this undercover profile easy to remember so he wouldn't slip and make a mistake that could give him away. But they still felt like foreign words on his tongue. That's why he liked to blend his fake persona with a little bit of reality—to make the role he had to play as real as possible. "My friends call me Duff."

"I'm not looking to make friends, Mr. Maynard." With a tone like that, she didn't have to worry. Surely, there'd be someone else at this place who'd be an easier mark for developing a relationship with to get the information he needed. He followed her to the cottage at the end of the crude neighborhood street and headed up the brick pathway bordered by colorful flowers. She pushed open the unlocked door and held it for Duff to enter before closing it behind him.

The blast of cool air that hit him after the heat and humidity outside raised goose bumps on his skin. For some reason he hadn't expected to find air-conditioning at this remote location. He sought out the source of the welcome chill in the steady hum of a window unit anchored over a small shelf crammed with books beside an empty brick fireplace. He used his survey to also identify a small dine-in kitchen area and a pair of open pinewood doors that led into a bedroom and a bathroom. The flowered love seat and white eyelet curtains at the front window seemed to indicate Melanie lived alone.

She dropped his bag beside the love seat. "Welcome to the infirmary."

"Quaint little place you've got here. Does everybody get his own house?"

"Married couples and families get their own place. Henry will probably put you up in the bachelor quarters near the equipment shed for now. You'll be able to eat meals there, too. Phyllis Schultz, who runs our bakery, cooks a big dinner for anyone who doesn't have his own kitchen."

"How did you luck out?" He nodded toward her left hand. "You're not married."

"No. I'm not. I doubt I'll ever be."

Now that was an odd addendum to make. Melanie Fiske might not be a beauty like her cousin, but the woman had fire and plenty of curves that would tempt the right man. *Not me*, he reminded himself. But even in this backwoods Eden, a woman in her midtwenties surely didn't think of herself as an old maid.

"I give people nicknames," he explained, telling himself not to be curious about what her cryptic comment might mean. "Baldy. Old Man. I ought to call you Red."

"You can call me Melanie," she drawled, slipping into that invisible armor again. Amusing him with her sass more than she knew, she opened a glass-paned door that was also hung with eyelet curtains for privacy off the west side of the tiny living room. "In here." She gestured to an examination table that looked as though it had come out of some old country doctor's office. "This is why I get to have my own place. Since I have to be on call around the clock, it makes sense to live in the quarters where all the medical supplies and sickbeds are kept."

He took in the two beds that were little more than metal cots made up with crisp white sheets and blankets, and the metal cabinets that were marred with rust around the hinges and corners. She washed her hands at a tiny porcelain sink before opening a dorm-size refrigerator and pulling out a vial of medicine. Then she opened drawers and the cabinet, which were, as she'd claimed, sparsely stocked and pulled out sterile gloves, alcohol, gauze bandages and a syringe packet. Duff was all for playing his part as a grizzled vet looking for some peace and quiet away from the crowds and noise of the city, but did he really want to get medical treatment from a woman who wasn't even a registered nurse, much less a doctor?

She faced him again, frowning when she saw he was still standing. "You're not afraid of needles, are you?"

He wasn't. Duff leaned his hip back against the table and sat. "You're sure you know what you're doing?"

Her chin came up and she pointed to the framed document on the wall. "I may not have all the medical training I'd like, but I have enough to do this job. There's my certification from the Metropolitan Community College in Kansas City."

So she'd been to school in KC. Someone commuting back and forth to classes could certainly smuggle a trunkful of guns into the city. He'd have to check to see if her schedule coincided with any of the suspected weapons deliveries. "When were you in Kansas City?"

But she wasn't interested in getting friendly. "We're talking a shot of topical anesthesia, cleaning the wound and eight, ten stitches, tops. I don't have antibiotics on hand to administer right now, but if you show signs of infection, there's a doctor in Falls City who does."

There was also a medical team on call for the task force. Duff would ask for one of those doctors to check him out when he made his scheduled report to his handler later tonight. In the meantime, if he thought about how confident her hands had felt checking his wound outside, and not how iffy the modernity of this infirmary might be, he had a surprising degree of confidence in her ability to heal him.

"Do your worst, Doc. I can take it." He reached for the hem of his T-shirt and peeled it off over his head, gingerly maneuvering the soiled material over his injured shoulder. By the time he'd wadded up the bloodied shirt and tossed it into the trash can, he had two big brown eyes staring at the center of his chest.

Well, I'll be damned. Melanie Fiske wasn't all cold and prickly and disinterested in men, after all. Although he could guess that a woman with medical training had seen a half-naked man before, her eyes seemed more than professionally curious about the particular dimensions of his bare chest and torso. He *was* built like a tank. Maybe she'd just never seen this much exposed male skin in her infirmary before.

"You, um—" she swallowed, and he watched the ripple of movement down her throat as a telltale blush moved in the opposite direction "—never answered my question about a tetanus shot. Is yours up-to-date?"

Maybe he could play off the innocence peeking through her tough tomboy facade and make a friend here, after all. "I'm good. That's one thing the army does right."

She tended to him for several minutes in silence, keeping her eyes carefully averted from bare-naked-chest land as she untied the bandanna and irrigated the wound. While she waited for the area where she'd given him the shot to grow numb, she shifted her attention to the tender swelling on his cheek and gently cleaned the scrape there. "How did it feel to punch Silas in the face?"

Interesting that that should be the first personal question she'd asked him. "Like it needed to be done."

"I can't tell you how often I wished I could…" Her fingers paused for a moment and he thought he glimpsed the dent of a dimple, indicating a brief smile before she went back to work. "I'm surprised he didn't pull the knife sooner. He hates to lose. Let me see your hands."

"They could use a little TLC. But I'll live."

After cleaning his hands and putting a bandage on one finger, she touched the boot-sized bruise on his flank. Duff sucked in a sharp breath as her fingers brushed across his skin. "Sorry." She'd thought she'd hurt him, but that eager response was all on him and the years he'd gone without a woman's tender touch. She prodded the skin all around the bruise, and Duff gritted his teeth at the exploration. "I'll get an ice pack. If it starts to swell, or you feel like you're struggling to breathe…"

She suddenly drew back her fingers. Had she maintained contact more than was medically necessary? Duff hadn't noticed. Or minded. Instead, he'd been thinking that the space between them smelled of the summer heat coming off her skin. And beneath the tinge of perspiration and antiseptic that lingered in the air, he detected a soft scent reminiscent of baby oil. That was her. The curvy tomboy with the plain features and wild auburn hair smelled like that. Sweet and down-to-earth, yet sexy—like she'd be soft to the touch if he reached out and brushed his fingertips across *her* skin. He hoped she wasn't one of the bad guys here. Because he was seriously tempted—

"I don't have an X-ray machine to check for internal injuries."

Now he was the one swallowing hard to regain his equilibrium. "I know what a cracked rib feels like. I'm breathing fine. This is just a bruise."

She pulled a tray of ice from the minifridge and wrapped the ice in a thin towel, placing it gently against his aching side. "You've been in a lot of fights?"

"A few."

"I'm sorry." She took his hand and placed it over the ice pack to hold it in place so that she could set up a tray with sutures. "That you've been hurt, I mean. I'm not sorry that somebody was able to put Silas in his place for once." She tilted her eyes up to his.

"Does that make me a bad person? That I feel like I should thank you?"

Maybe the woman was more bluff than any real experience with men. Since she wasn't attached to anyone here, he could take advantage of her apparent interest in him. She seemed to be at odds with Henry Fiske, but she was part of his family. And, clearly, she had some kind of history with Danvers. She'd know everyone here and have access to most, if not all, of the facilities. And this conversation was giving him the feeling that he could get close to her, after all.

For a split second, Shayla Ortiz's face superimposed itself over Melanie's. He'd used her, too, to get close to her drug-dealing brother. And that had turned into the worst sort of disaster an undercover cop could face. He'd lost his focus on the case when he'd fallen in love. Shayla had betrayed him and blown his cover to protect herself, and he hadn't seen it coming until it was too late.

But Duff was a decade older and wiser now. He didn't have to trust Melanie Fiske—he just had to make her think he did. He had to make her believe he cared about her. He didn't have the suave charm of his youngest brother to draw on, but how sophisticated could a woman who'd grown up in the boonies of Missouri be? She just needed somebody to be nicer to her than Danvers had been, and that wouldn't be much of a challenge. If he paid attention to a few details, he could figure out what was important to her and pretend those things were important to him, too.

Melanie tucked a damp tendril behind her ear and held it there as her freckled cheeks colored with a rosy blush. "I guess that makes me a hypocrite—trying to stop the violence, yet wishing I could have done it myself."

Duff realized he'd been staring long enough to make her uncomfortable—just the opposite of what he needed to be doing if he was going to woo her into becoming an ally. He ignored the stab of guilt that tried to warn him away from involving her in his investigation. "Has Danvers given you trouble before? Do you know how to fight?"

"So far I've relied on outwitting him. It isn't that hard."

Duff wanted to grin at her sarcasm, but the fact that the man who'd cut his arm open had threatened her, as well, didn't sit well with him. "I could give you a few pointers on defending yourself."

"You'd teach me to fight." Now that was a skeptical look. "Like you were doing out there with Silas?"

Realistically, he doubted she could take Silas down the same way he had. But there were ways. "You just have to be smarter than your opponent, do the unexpected and be fierce about committing to the attack. I could show you escape maneuvers—and you probably already know some of the key targets if you want to incapacitate a man."

Her gaze dropped down to the zipper of his jeans and up to the column of his throat.

"I see you already know a couple of vulnerable spots." He really should feel guilty about saying things that triggered that graphic response on her skin. Instead, he was wondering what else he could say or do to make her skin color like that.

She quickly averted her face. "I'd appreciate that. If you have the time."

Her hip brushed against his thigh as she inserted the first stitch. Duff turned his nose to the crown of her hair, inhaling the scents of baby shampoo and damp summer heat. "I'll make the time for you."

"You don't even know your work schedule…" Before she made the next stitch, she tipped her face to his. Her breath caught with an audible startle at how close he was to her, but Duff made no effort to retreat.

Her eyes weren't ordinary at all. Their cool brown color, spiked with flecks of amber, reminded him of the fine Irish whiskey he and his brothers liked to sip on special occasions. With her sweet scent and eyes like that, he wouldn't have to pretend that this woman had some pretty about her, after all.

"When I say I'm going to do a thing, I do it."

He lowered his gaze to the quiver of her lips and felt a twist of hunger low in his belly. He could kiss her right now if he wanted to. Maybe the bold move would shock her into kissing him back. Or she might just slap his face for doing without asking.

"Don't make promises you can't keep." Her hands were suddenly very busy with the cut on his shoulder.

"I don't."

Yep. Busy, busy. She didn't know what to do about her interest in him. She didn't know how to hide it, either. As long as he didn't spook her, he could give her a few lessons about how to indulge that awareness she was feeling. And, damn it, he was going to take advantage of that attraction. Because the mission required it.

But that meant ignoring his conscience and his errant libido, and taking it slow so he wouldn't frighten her off before he had the chance to solidify a connection between them. So he dialed back his own curiosity about what her lips might taste like and thought about the vanishing man who'd shot his grandfather and the reason he was here in the first place. Duff set the ice pack on the bed beside him and captured a strand of Melanie's auburn hair, pulling it away from the damp spot on her left breast. The kinky tendril was thick and soft as he rubbed it between his thumb and fingers, stirring up the scents he'd noticed earlier. She must use baby products for all her personal toiletries. If he needed any further testament to her innocence...

Melanie pulled away at the same moment he forgot that touching her was supposed to be an act.

"Give me a sec." She exited the room for a minute or so, and came back in, sans the blush, tying a rubber band around the long braid that hung over her shoulder. Without another word, she pulled on a new pair of sterile gloves and prepped the needle for the next stitch. Her tough-chick armor was back in place.

But Duff wasn't about to surrender the opportunity to get closer to her. "That's a shame, winding up all that wild hair like that." He reached out and twisted the heavy braid between his fingers, using it to tug her into the vee of his legs. "I liked it better down."

Chapter Four

"You liked…?" Melanie caught her breath when the back of Tom Maynard's knuckles brushed across her breast as he played with the braid of her hair. The caress tingled over her skin, tightening the tip into a tender pearl. Was that an accident? Or had that touch been intentional? She cringed at the sound of denim rasping against denim. She was nestled between his thighs and she wasn't making any effort to move away from the warmth surrounding her.

"Are you hitting on me?" With an awkward push and a nearly stifling amount of embarrassed heat creeping up to her cheeks, she stepped around his knee. A half-sewn suture linking her hands to his shoulder kept her from bolting across the room. "You'll make me mess up this stitch."

She'd been stripped down to wet undies that were transparent to the skin an hour or so ago and hadn't felt as exposed as she did fully dressed with Tom Maynard. Of course, no one had touched her, accidentally or otherwise, when she'd been swimming in her skivvies. And this man seemed to keep finding reasons to touch her. Where was that sharp tongue she'd used to tell off Silas and her uncle? Was she really so starved for some tender attention from a man that she'd forget her vow to steer clear of any entanglements on the farm?

She stopped herself from reaching inside her pocket again to touch her father's watch. It was a superstitious habit, really, thinking that holding on to the busted watch could bring back either of her parents. The scratched-up piece of gold couldn't really channel her father's spirit and give her clarity and reassurance when she needed it. She had to be smart enough to remember all the life lessons her widowed father had taught her right up until the night he'd died.

Except that she'd been a girl of eleven when Leroy Fiske had drowned. And, somehow, the lessons she'd learned as a little girl never included how she was supposed to react to a man who stirred things inside her. Even when he didn't mean to. Or did he? She'd been secretly cheering for Tom Maynard when he'd stood up to Henry and Silas's authority. They'd had to gang up on Tom and pull a weapon to turn the tide of power back in their favor. For a few moments, she thought she'd found her hero—the perfect ally—a way out of the nightmare unfolding around her these past few months. No wonder she'd been so eager to defy her uncle's authority and step into the middle of a fight.

Then she realized he was going to be like the other men here—overlooking her uncle's lies and accepting his questionable dictates in exchange for a share of the farm's profits—or whatever a man like Tom needed.

But the promise of a hero must have lingered inside her because she'd been ogling Tom's imposing chest and the T-shaped dusting of brown hair that tapered into a line that disappeared beneath his belt buckle, imagining being held close to all that muscle and heat again. Did her reaction to his touch mean she liked Tom? Had catching her admiring the muscular landscape sent her patient the message that she wanted to be touched? If so, how did she change that message? Because it really wasn't in her plans right now to...to what? Make a friend? Have an affair? Completely embarrass herself by revealing that she'd reached the age of twenty-five with more experience fishing than kissing?

"Hey, Doc, you okay?" His voice rumbled in a drowsy timbre. "You got quiet on me."

She hated how her skin telegraphed every emotion, putting her at a disadvantage when she couldn't read whatever Tom was thinking or feeling. "I did?" She cleared her throat to mask the embarrassingly breathless quality of her own voice. "I'm sorry. What were we talking about?"

"Why you tamed all that hair into a braid like this. You've sure got a lot of it." Was that supposed to be a compliment? Or a remark about how the Missouri humidity could wreak havoc on too much naturally curly hair? And, goodness, was he still twirling the tail end of her braid between his fingers?

She couldn't summon her father's spirit to guide

her, but she could muster up a little common sense. Melanie pulled the braid from his fingers and swung it behind her back. "It's not practical to have it flying all over the place when I have to do work like this. I can't tell you how many times I've been tempted to cut it all off."

"Now *that* would be a shame. It's like earthy fire."

Melanie lowered her needle and tipped her gaze past the brown stubble dusting his jaw to meet his smiling green eyes. "Is that your best line? That *is* a line, isn't it?" She understood a brute like Silas pawing at her and barking orders more than she ever had men who pretended she was pretty or special so that they could get something from her. And this man with his neat military haircut and unshaven face, his mature body and boyish grin, his eagerness to fight *and* flirt, definitely wanted something. "You give people nicknames because refusing to use their real name is a way to put distance between you. I'm not a doctor, so stop calling me Doc. You told Henry that you wanted to get away from people, and yet you're trying to make friends with me. I need you to watch where you put your hands, and my hair is *earthy fire*? What does that even mean? If you want to say something, just say it. I don't understand why men can't be honest."

He put up his hands in surrender. "Whoa, sweetheart. I think I just got lumped in with some bad history. You don't even know me. Not all men are dishonest."

She wanted to believe that. But, after a few run-ins with her uncle and Silas, she doubted it. She got a sense that even this one who'd protected her from Silas's knife was lying about something.

"And I'll start keeping my hands to myself once you stop putting yours on me," he said.

"I'm treating your injury."

"That's not all you're doing, Doc."

Melanie groaned as he teased her with the nickname again.

"Sure, I'm trying to be friendly," he said. "We're going to be seeing each other almost every day, right? And giving you those self-defense lessons? Trust me, they'll go easier if you don't think of me as the enemy. You gotta give me a chance."

She knocked his left hand down and moved closer to sew another stitch. "No, I don't."

His arm flinched against his side and he swore. "Easy, Doc—er, Mel. Melanie. *Miss Fiske.*" That snippy tone of mockery she understood. "That one pinched."

She stopped before cutting the end of the suture, appalled that she'd let this man's teasing and touching, and her own distrustful thoughts, get in the way of her doing her job with the care and accuracy in which she prided herself. No matter what her issues were with her uncle, she had no right to take her frustration out on a patient. "I'm sorry." She quickly analyzed the neat row of stitches to make sure she hadn't aggravated his injury. "Did I hurt you?"

"I'll live. But I felt the tug." He dipped his square

jaw to line up his gaze with hers. "Why are you so mad at me? I figured you'd be grateful."

"For what?"

"Danvers was more than happy to cut you, as well as me. I got you out of there."

"I thought I got *you* out of there."

"You do like to argue a point. How is that any different than me giving you a nickname? You're workin' awfully hard to keep your distance from me, too." He scrubbed his fingers over the top of his hair, leaving a trail of short spikes sticking up in a dozen different directions. "When I think you might actually like me."

"Whatever gave you that idea?"

He traced her collarbone around the neckline of her T-shirt. "That blush creepin' up your neck."

Melanie's hand flew to her throat as he pulled his finger away, grinning at her inability to hide the truth. "I don't know you well enough to decide whether or not I like you."

He sat back on the table. "You're not even going to give me a chance to find out if we can get along?"

"I thought you told Henry that you were here for peace and quiet—that you wanted to be left alone."

Grim lines appeared beside his eyes as his teasing smile faded. "I get a little paranoid in a crowd—but I do pretty good one-on-one."

What kind of *good* was he talking about? A good friend? A good boyfriend? The wannabe nurse or doctor in her tempered her determination to resist him. This man was a veteran, after all. With the few hints he'd dropped already, he was probably suffering from some degree of post-traumatic stress. Maybe he was reaching out to her because he felt safe with her. Maybe he saw some kind of kinship with her already because she'd jumped in on his side of the fight when no one else had. It kind of made sense. He probably didn't see her as any threat. "That's all you want? A chance?"

"That's all a man ever wants." The angry lines softened. And though the teasing smile didn't reappear, he dropped his voice to a growly whisper that indicated some sort of intimacy. "Unless he's one of those jackasses who's lied to you."

Men didn't talk softly to her. And they certainly didn't share anything that resembled intimacy. The hard walls of defense she'd lived with every day since finding her father's watch crumbled just a little bit. Remembering the professional training she prided herself on, Mel placed the ice pack in Tom's hand and guided it up to the violet-red mark on his cheekbone. "All right, then. We can try to be friends. But maybe you shouldn't talk for a while. I'll finish faster if you let me concentrate on my work."

"In other words, zip it?"

He held her gaze until she nodded. Then he looked away, ostensibly taking in every corner of her mismatched but clean treatment room. A crooked smile softened the square line of his jaw, and she had to tamp down those little frissons of infatuation that tried to take hold of her again. She wouldn't say Tom Maynard was handsome, exactly. But he was overtly male in a way that woke up feminine impulses inside her that she'd ignored for a very long time.

But ignore them she would. She was agreeing to a trial friendship—nothing more. Making sure to gentle her touch, Melanie sewed in the last few stitches until the blood oozing from the wound had completely stopped. She inspected the neat line of the mended cut and cleaned the area again before opening the antibiotic ointment and prepping the gauze and adhesive tape to cover it.

"Out of all the men you've ever known, every last one of them has lied to you?"

Tom's deep voice startled her as much as the probing question. Melanie fumbled the roll of tape she'd been using and it rolled away underneath the sink. Glad she could move away from the distracting body heat that even the air-conditioning couldn't seem to diminish, she got down on her hands and knees to retrieve it. "In my experience, they say what they want you to hear. Or else they make stuff up because they think it's what *I* want to hear. Like saying I'm pretty when I know I'm not." She stood and returned the tape to its spot inside the barren storage cabinet. "Half the men around here think that sweet-talking me will get them closer to Henry. Or to my cousin, Deanna. Every single man here has his eye on her. And why not? She's gorgeous and outgoing, easy to like. She eats up the attention."

"Danvers was hitting on *you* when he mentioned that dance."

"He was asserting his authority and assuaging

his pride. If he thought dating one of the dairy cows in the south pasture would secure his position with Henry, he'd do it."

Tom chuckled, and the warm laugh sounded genuine enough to make her want to smile in return. "You've got a pretty wicked sense of humor when you're not busy pushing people away." He drew a cross over his heart with his finger. "No lie."

Keeping her smile to herself at the childish gesture, Melanie carried the soiled supplies to the trash. She peeled off her gloves and tossed them, too, before facing her patient again. "My father was an honest man."

"Was?"

"He died when I was eleven."

"I'm sorry." The lines of sun and stress reappeared beside his eyes as he narrowed his gaze. "Your mom?"

"Why do you ask?"

"That's how you make friends. You ask questions and get to know a person. So does your mom live here?"

Melanie shook her head. "She died when I was born. There were complications. The midwife couldn't stop the bleeding, and Dad couldn't get her to the hospital in time. It's what motivated me to get emergency medical training. When something like that happens, it feels like we're a long way from civilization out here."

"That's rough."

She took the ice pack from him and emptied it

before draping the towel over the edge of the sink. "It wasn't all bad. I have wonderful memories of Dad. He taught me about the trees and wildlife here, how to run a fishing boat. He told me all about my mother, read to me at night. He took me swimming, hiking, canoeing..."

And then she couldn't talk about it anymore. Not with the fear that something horrible had happened to her father, and she'd never suspected—never even thought to suspect—a crime, or at least a cover-up, until just a few months ago. With the grit of unwanted tears stinging her eyes, Melanie excused herself to retrieve Tom's bag from her living room. She lifted the sleeve of her T-shirt and dabbed it against her eyes until she'd replaced sorrow and guilt with the determination to do right by her father.

"So Henry and Abby raised you." She jumped as Tom palmed the small of her back and reached around her to pick up his bag before she could reach it. "Sorry. Gotta work on that hands-to-myself thing. So, no nicknames, no touching, and any time I have a conversation with you, I need to be brutally honest."

Melanie was still gaping with surprise. She hadn't even heard him follow her into the room. "I prefer that."

"All right, then. I'll tell you something real about me."

Manners aside, the man didn't have much to do with modesty, either. He unhooked his belt and slipped on the knife Silas had taken from him before digging inside the bag a second time to pull out a rolled-up black T-shirt. When he reached for the zipper of his jeans, she turned away to face the eyelet curtains at her front window.

"My mom was murdered when I was in high school," he said. "By a couple of druggies robbing a convenience store where she'd gone to pick up milk."

"Oh, my God." She turned right back. "That's awful. I'm so sorry." If he was trying to gain her sympathy or show they had something in common, he might be succeeding. She understood that lonesome ache, that empty space in her heart where unconditional love used to reside. Did he? Could he truly understand how torn she was inside—wanting to get away from this place that had caused her such pain, yet needing to stay and do whatever was necessary to uncover the truth? She waited for him to pull on the shirt so she could read the sincerity of his expression. But it was the same craggy face with the same unreadable green eyes that she'd seen earlier. "Is that true?"

He carefully adjusted his sleeve over the gauze bandage before tucking in the hem and fastening his jeans and belt. He pulled his gun from the bag and slipped it on over his shoulders, completing the look of a warrior before his gaze settled on hers. "I never lie about my mama."

There was a hard edge to his eyes and mouth and even in his posture that made her believe he was telling the truth. She tightened her grip around the end of her braid, fighting off the impulse to reach out and offer some sort of comfort. Right now, though, he didn't look like the sort of man who needed or wanted comfort. This was what a soldier who'd seen too much looked like. This was the man who wanted a job away from the bustle of too many people, too many buildings, too much noise. This glimpse of what she suspected the real Tom Maynard was like beneath the crude charm and nicknames was, frankly, a little scary. But she'd take this *brutal* honesty over sweet-talking lies any day. Maybe she could use an ally like that in her quest to find the truth. Not that she could ever fully trust him—not while he worked for Henry. "I'm sorry about your mother. Did the police find her killer?"

"Yes."

"You found closure after her death?"

"I guess." The steely set of his shoulders relaxed with a heavy exhalation, and he knelt to pick up the flannel shirt and balled-up socks that had fallen from his bag and stuffed them inside. "I'll always be pissed off at the lowlife who shot her, and I'll always miss her. But it happened a long time ago, and the shooter and his partner will be in prison for the rest of their lives, so, yeah, I guess that's closure." With a firm tug, he cinched the bag shut and pushed to his feet. "Why do you ask?"

She wanted the same kind of justice for her father— or proof beyond a reasonable doubt that Leroy's death *had* been an accident. Maybe her uncle had found the watch on the boat after it had been towed ashore, and he'd simply helped himself to the memento of his brother. But if there was a sentimental reason for keeping it, why stuff it in a forgotten box in the attic? Other relatives had swarmed in to take things that had belonged to her father—as a child, she'd been helpless to stop them. As a grown-up, she wondered if any of their motives had been sentimental—or if taking pretty much anything that wasn't nailed down had held a more sinister purpose. As much as she felt compassion for Tom's loss of a parent, she wasn't ready to share her suspicions with a stranger. It was dangerous to share them with anyone around here.

Instead, she countered with a question of her own. "Why did you tell me about your mother?"

"You asked for a truth. And that's one I'm willing to share." So there were other truths he didn't intend to tell her? "You want to know another one?" He pointed to her left ear. "You've got a kink of hair stickin' up like a horn on the side of your head." Her hand immediately flew there. She snagged the wayward strand and stuffed it into place behind her ear. A slow grin spread across his face, breaking the somber mood. "But I do love the color of it. I don't know if I've ever touched red hair before. And this is the real deal, isn't it?" He caught the braid she'd been fidgeting with a few moments earlier and held it up in his palm to study it. "Don't know why I thought it'd feel different from any other color. Is that honest enough for you?"

Melanie tugged the braid from his fingers and, this time, despite her best effort, she smiled back. "I don't know what to make of you, Tom. I can't tell if you're trying to shock me or seduce me."

He arched an eyebrow. "Is that second one an option?"

Melanie was silently cursing the embarrassing heat crawling up her neck when someone knocked on her front door.

"Mel? Are you in here?" The door swung open before Melanie could reach it. A wave of hot air rushed in, followed by very pregnant blonde woman.

"SueAnn?" She took one look at her friend's pale cheeks and grabbed hold of her arm. Melanie kicked the door shut and guided her into the living room, unsure if this was a friendly visit or a medical one. "Did you run over here? Are you all right? Is the baby okay?"

Rubbing her heavy belly, SueAnn Renick wheezed for breath and leaned against Mel. "Is he here? I heard you had a patient. Is it Richard?" Tom lifted his duffel bag out of her path and SueAnn tilted her head back to greet him. "You're the new guy?"

"Yes, ma'am. Duff Maynard."

Melanie urged her to sit. "I thought I told you to stay inside during the heat of the day. Catch your breath and I'll get you a glass of water."

But SueAnn rolled to her feet and tottered right after her. "I heard you were treating an injured man. Is Richard okay?"

"Richard isn't here." Melanie turned to see her panicked friend swaying on her feet and quickly linked her arm through hers to walk her toward the infirmary door. "I was taking care of Tom. You need to relax. I'll get you a cool compress."

"I know I'm really emotional with the baby. But I have a right to be, don't I?" SueAnn moved her hand from her belly up to her forehead to lift her sunny gold bangs off her face.

Melanie couldn't tell if that was perspiration or tears beading on her friend's cheeks. But she could tell the woman was overheated and dangerously close to hyperventilating. "Of course, you do. But Richard's a grown man who can take care of himself. You need to think of yourself and the baby right now."

"How can I? What if he's in trouble and needs me? It's been four months since he left. A man doesn't get a job just a few miles away and never return home. We've always been close. He'd call or send a letter if he could, wouldn't he?" SueAnn braced her hand against the doorjamb and stopped. She looked inside the empty infirmary, then back up to the armed man still standing in the middle of Melanie's living room. Her breath rushed out in a sharp gasp. "Oh. He's your patient. I guess I wasn't thinking straight."

"Sorry to disappoint you." Tom stepped forward and extended his hand. "Like I said, I'm Duff. Is everything all right, ma'am? Who's Richard?"

"My brother." She shook his hand. "I'm the one who should apologize. SueAnn Renick. Resident crazy lady."

Melanie tried to get her moving again. "Tom, you'd better go."

"I know something's wrong." She spun, grabbing on to Melanie's arm with a sweaty palm as the color drained from her face. "Something's happened to

Richard. It's this horrible place. He saw his chance to leave and…" She rocked back against the wall. "I am feeling a little light-headed…" She cradled her belly and slid toward the floor.

Chapter Five

Melanie barely had time to cradle her friend's head and keep it from hitting the wall when a blur of black shirt and big shoulders nudged her aside.

"I've got her." Tom caught SueAnn in his arms and tipped the unconscious woman against his chest.

"Be careful of your stitches," Melanie warned.

Without so much as a grunt of discomfort, he pushed to his feet, lifting her pregnant friend. "What's wrong with her?"

"Put her in here and let me check." Pushing aside the fleeting thought that Tom Maynard seemed to have a knack for rescuing women, Melanie pointed to the nearest cot. SueAnn's blackout had been only temporary, but the woman was still woozy from the heat, exertion and fear that had brought her running in a few minutes earlier. Once Tom had laid her on the cool sheets, he backed up to let Melanie work. While she wrapped a blood-pressure cuff around SueAnn's arm, she nodded toward the sink. "Grab that wet towel and fold it up for me."

Thankfully, he was quick to obey the order. He

handed her a neat compress that was still cool from the melted ice. "You really are the doctor around here."

"I wish." She sat on the edge of the cot and placed the compress on SueAnn's forehead. The frantic woman's blue eyes opened, then drifted shut again.

"Is she all right?"

Melanie plugged the stethoscope into her ears and listened to the rapid beat of SueAnn's pulse. Her blood pressure had spiked to 160/100. Not good. Melanie shook her head and pointed to the file cabinet across the room. "Look under *R* for Renick and pull SueAnn's file. I'll need a pen, too." As eager to help now as he'd been a recalcitrant patient himself, Tom brought her the requested items. She listened to the baby's heartbeat, as well as SueAnn's, before adding the vitals to the record she was keeping. She was seeing a pattern here that was as troubling as the idea of secrets surrounding her father's death.

She moved the compress to SueAnn's neck and wrists, trying to cool the pulse points. "She's worried about her brother. He's been missing for several weeks."

"Missing?" Tom's shadow towered beside her. "Did you report it to the sheriff?"

The disappearance of Richard Lloyd wasn't Melanie's main concern. "SueAnn, you need to see a real doctor. I can't control these blood-pressure spikes without medication. They're not safe for you or the baby."

SueAnn blinked her eyes open. "Our home is here. This is where I want to raise my baby."

"That doesn't mean you shouldn't go to a hospital to deliver him or her. A real doctor could tell you if it *is* a him or her. You need to go to Henry and ask him to let you and Daryl go to Falls City or, better yet, Kansas City."

"He'll never agree to that." She dropped her voice to a nervous whisper and glanced up at Tom. "Besides, you know Daryl can't get a job that pays as well anywhere else. And if we leave, how will Richard find us when he comes home?" Melanie felt her friend's pulse beating faster beneath her fingertips. SueAnn swatted aside the compress and pushed herself up on her elbows. If it weren't for her awkward balance and Melanie blocking her way, she would have climbed right off the cot and probably fainted again. "You don't think Sheriff Cobb put him in jail for getting drunk again, do you? What could he have done to keep him imprisoned all these weeks?"

"We don't know that he's in jail. The sheriff would have said something. Richard would have been given a phone call."

"I just know something terrible has happened to him." SueAnn gulped in a sob of breath and fought against Melanie's helping hands.

"Ma'am? SueAnn?" A deep voice sounded beside Melanie as Tom knelt beside her. His big hands replaced Melanie's on the other woman's shoulders and lowered her to the bed. "You need to think of your baby. Take deep breaths." He inhaled and exhaled along with her. "That's it. Now why don't you tell me a little bit about this brother of yours."

Melanie stared at the jut of Tom's shoulder moving between her and her patient, eyeing the strip of white adhesive tape peeking out between his tanned skin and the snug fit of his sleeve. He was certainly a man of contrasts, able to handle the violence of a fight as easily as he comforted a hysterical woman. Melanie should suspect his motives for still being here when he could have left several minutes ago, but right now she was grateful for the soothing resonance of his voice and the calming effect it seemed to have on SueAnn.

Encouraging Tom to take her place on the edge of the cot, Melanie got up. "I'll get her something to drink."

She pulled out a fresh towel and ran it beneath the faucet while SueAnn rattled on. "His name's Richard. The night before he left he told me he was taking on an extra job in town. Henry had arranged it. Or maybe it was Silas. I can't seem to remember. A lot of the men pick up extra work when money's tight around here."

"Is money tight?" Tom was frowning when Melanie glanced back at him. "I thought this looked like a pretty prosperous place."

"Did you come from Falls City? Did you see a young man with blond hair?"

Tom shook his head. "I was just passin' through when I met Mr. Fiske and got word about a job doing nighttime security work here."

"Night security?" SueAnn collapsed against her pillow. "That used to be Richard's job. I wonder if he borrowed money from Henry. He had that new truck when he left. Maybe he thought he had to take the job in order to pay Henry back."

"Do you know what kind of job he had?" Tom asked. "Or what kind of truck he was driving? I could go back to Falls City and look for him."

"Enough. She needs rest." Melanie pressed the damp towel to SueAnn's lips. "Here. Suck some water out of it if you can."

Her front door swung open to the clump of footsteps and a deep, worried shout. "SueAnn!"

Daryl Renick dashed through the infirmary door before Melanie could meet him. He pushed a heavy box into her arms and moved right past her, eyeing Tom away from his wife and taking his place at the side of the bed. He tossed his shaggy brown hair out of his eyes and captured SueAnn's hand between his. "Honey, I heard you were in the clinic. Is everything okay? Did something happen with the baby?"

"It was just a silly mistake. I'll be fine."

Daryl smoothed SueAnn's bangs off her face and pressed a kiss to her forehead. He rested his palm on her distended belly before raising his dark eyes to Melanie's. "Silas didn't do something stupid to scare her, did he? I got those disposable phones he asked for."

Tom frowned. "Why would Silas want to scare your wife?"

Melanie jumped in when she saw Daryl's deerin-the-headlight expression. She wouldn't put it past Silas to coerce someone into doing what he wanted, and, clearly, Daryl's trip into Falls City hadn't all been about fetching medical supplies. She set the box of supplies on the exam table before offering him a rueful smile. "SueAnn passed out in my living room." She nodded toward the muscular man lurking in the doorway. "Tom brought her in and helped me calm her down. But she needs to see a doctor."

"I know it." Daryl extended a hand to Tom and nodded to Melanie, including them both in his thanks. "Thank you. I'll talk to Henry again about visiting that specialist in Kansas City."

"I don't need Dr. Ayres." Despite her wan color, SueAnn was all smiles now as she reached out to Melanie. "You're all we need, Mel. You've taken care of me for eight months. You'll take good care of my baby, too. You delivered Alice's baby."

Melanie took her friend's hand. "One baby doesn't make me an expert. What if there are complications?"

SueAnn gave her hand a weak squeeze. "Then I know you will fight harder to save my baby—and me—than anyone else. I believe in you."

Maybe she shouldn't. Melanie gently squeezed back before releasing her hand. "You rest here for a while. Daryl, you stay with her. Make sure she drinks some more water."

"I will."

Melanie led Tom out of the infirmary and closed the door. But her frustration erupted in a noisy groan as she stormed across the room to pull out the obstetrics textbook she'd been poring over these past few weeks.

Tom planted himself in the middle of the room while she turned to the index and searched for the information she wanted to double-check. "If she needs to see a regular doctor, why doesn't she just go?"

"Things are complicated around here. Henry and Abby—they make deals. They do nice things for people. But they expect loyalty in return." She set the open book on top of the shelf and flipped through the pages. "They helped Daryl and SueAnn get a house. The yellow one at the end of the lane."

"I saw it. Looks like a new build. That's a pretty expensive bribe to ensure someone's loyalty."

"Daryl spent time in prison for stealing cars. He served his time and all—before he met SueAnn. She knows his background, and he's so good to her. But it's been hard for them to get credit anywhere because of his record."

"So your uncle bought him the house. And now Daryl owes him. They have to stay."

She paused in the middle of skimming the page and turned. Maybe it wasn't too late for Tom to do the smart thing and get out of here. "Henry worries that if people leave, they won't come back. Like SueAnn's brother. Richard left the farm four months ago, and we haven't seen him since. He's a screwup sometimes, probably drinks more than he should, but I can't believe he'd upset his sister like this."

"A man doesn't disappear for no reason." Tom

splayed his hands at his waist, drawing her attention to the gun, the knife and the threat of danger that emanated from his very posture. "He either doesn't want to be found—or something's keeping him from contacting the people he cares about."

"You want to disappear."

"I've got a reason."

She supposed he did if he suffered from PTSD. But the Richard Lloyd she knew was a different sort of man. "Richard likes to have a good time and laugh and be with people. He and Daryl hunt and fish all the time. He's a relentless flirt, even though every girl around here knows not to take him seriously. I can't see him ever wanting to be alone like you do."

"You're that worried about SueAnn and her brother?"

Melanie turned back to her textbook to recheck the information she'd already memorized. But she wasn't a physician and she didn't have access to any of those medications. "I used to think this was an idyllic place. Life was simple, but productive. I was honoring my father's legacy by staying here and helping the farm become a success." She closed the heavy book, feeling helpless to fix anyone's problems. "Now things are so..."

"So what?" Before she realized he'd even crossed the room, Tom's fingers wrapped around her elbow. He turned her to face him, leaving Melanie no place to retreat. "Is there something going on here I need to know about before I join the team? What did Henry do to ensure your loyalty?"

Didn't the man have any notion of personal space? His shoulders blocked her view of the infirmary, and every breath she took was tinged with the scents of musky heat and antiseptic coming off his skin.

She tilted up her chin to meet the scrutiny in his moss-colored eyes. She probably shouldn't tell him how much she was questioning her loyalty to her uncle right now. "He paid for my schooling and the expenses of living in Kansas City for a year and a half. He put a roof over my head and raised me after Dad's death. I should be grateful."

"Should be?"

That was a stupid slip of the tongue. "I *am* grateful. The Ozarks are a beautiful place to grow up. And I always wanted to do something in the field of medicine. I owe that to him."

"But?"

Melanie flattened her hand in the middle of his chest and pushed him back a step so she could think and breathe properly. "Why can't you just accept the answers I give you? Why does every answer lead to another question?"

"Because I don't think you're telling me everything."

And she wasn't about to. No matter how tempting his strength and penchant for rescuing a damsel in distress might be, she didn't really know Tom—*my friends call me Duff*—Maynard. If she didn't trust the people she knew well around here, why should she trust an outsider?

But Tom had protected her from Silas's temper

and helped SueAnn, and she had silently agreed to make the effort to be his friend, so she settled for sharing a different truth. Turning her back to him, she picked up the textbook and hugged it to her chest. "I wish I could get out of this place and go back to school again. I'm trained for basic medical procedures and illnesses—not a hypertensive pregnant woman who may need an emergency C-section. I'm reading everything I can to help SueAnn. But it's not the same as having the real experience and a sterile operating room."

The creak of leather in his belt or holster was the only sound to give him away as he moved in beside her. He ran his fingertip across the spines of the top row of books. "Have you read all these?"

"Why have books if you're not going to read them?"

He pulled out her tattered copy of *Jane Eyre*, checking the last page number and frowning before handing it over to her. "You liked going to school?"

"I take it you didn't?"

"I got through it well enough to play football and graduate. But the classwork wasn't really my thing."

She plucked the novel from his hand before sliding both books back into their places on the shelf. "I came home to work off the debt I owed my aunt and uncle since they paid for my classes. But I'd go back to school in a heartbeat if I could—back to KC to finish my nursing or even premed degree."

"I grew up in KC."

Melanie's pulse picked up at that casual pronouncement. "You know Kansas City?"

"Chiefs football. Jazz. Barbecue." He glanced
around her humble home with its handwoven throw
rugs and rustic decor. "I guess I figured you lived
out here all your life. The city traffic didn't scare
you? You weren't overwhelmed by all the crowds
and noise?"

Melanie shook her head. The city had been an
exciting place for her. She'd made friends, and had
learned so much about so many things beyond her
books and professors and practicums. This could be
dangerous territory for her, finding one more thing
she had in common with Tom. "What was your favorite part of KC?"

"I guess I never really thought about it before,"
he said.

"I loved exploring it," she gushed. "The Plaza
lights on Thanksgiving night. Union Station and its
science center. The museums. Maybe there's something in my genes. I've got an ancestor who was a
wagon-train master on the Santa Fe Trail. I grew up
learning all the waterways and trees and paths around
these hills. The city just has different terrain—and a
different sort of wildlife."

He arched an eyebrow at that comment, making
her wonder if she sounded foolish to him. But she
wasn't going to apologize for possessing a sense of ad-
venture. She wasn't ashamed of hoping for something
better than the life she had here. "I'm going back to

Kansas City to finish my degree one day. When the time is right, nobody will be able to stop me."

"When the time is right?" Those sharp green eyes seemed to be reading more into this conversation than she wanted him to. "If you've got a dream that big, why don't you go for it? You can get a job, scholarships, loans if money's the issue."

"I have other reasons for staying here."

He nodded toward the infirmary door. "Like your friend?"

"Somebody has to take care of SueAnn."

"You put your dreams on hold for a friend?"

And a father.

He captured the tendril of hair that must have sprung free again and tucked the independent lock behind her ear. Why did this man keep finding reasons to touch her? And why wasn't she protesting his boldness?

"You are one surprise after another, Doc."

Melanie groaned at the teasing misnomer. "I told you I wasn't—"

Her front door swung open without so much as a knock and Silas Danvers strolled in. Although she was expected to keep her door unlocked during the day in case there was a medical emergency, she was thinking seriously about installing a dead bolt on her door. "Don't tell me you're hurt now, too."

The bruise swelling around his cheek and left eye said he was, but that wasn't why he was here. She interpreted Silas's clean shirt and too-busy-for-niceties glare as a no. "I heard Daryl was back. He didn't check in. Is he here?"

Tom beat her to the infirmary door, planting himself in Silas's path. "His wife wasn't feeling well. Give them a few minutes."

"Was I talking to you? I need to know if he got everything on the list I sent with him."

"What list is that?" When Tom rolled his shoulders as if he was willing to go another round with Silas, Melanie tapped his forearm and urged him to step aside.

With eight new stitches in his arm, he didn't need to be going another round with anybody. She didn't want a fight in her home, and she certainly didn't want these two in a ruckus that would upset SueAnn further. "It's okay. He can go in."

Now why had she turned to Tom for help in averting an argument? Was she so certain Silas wouldn't listen to her that anyone else would make a better ally? Or was she really buying into Tom's efforts to become her friend? With a glance down to where her hand touched his skin, Tom nodded and stepped away.

Silas must have interpreted his response to her request as a sign of weakness. Smirking, he brushed past Tom and opened the door. "Meet me on the porch of the main house. I'll show you where you can bunk and park your rig." He eyed the leather straps of Tom's holster. "And find a less conspicuous way to wear that gun. You'll scare the tourists."

"You get a lot of visitors on the property after

dark?" Tom's question was riddled with sarcasm. Silas closed the door with only a sneer for an answer. "I'm glad I punched him in the face, too. Guess that's my exit cue."

Melanie followed as he scooped up his duffel bag and swung it onto his uninjured shoulder. "Thanks for helping with SueAnn. And for sharing about your mother."

"Thanks for puttin' me back together, Doc." He put up a hand in apology at using the nickname. "I know. Can't seem to help myself. You can call me Duff if it'll make you feel better."

"We'll see." Melanie opened the door for him. "What does Duff mean, anyway?"

"Oh, now that I'm leaving, she's interested. Meet me again sometime, and I'll tell you." He stepped outside. "You know, maybe you've got it all backward with that nickname rule. I don't think it has anything to do with putting distance between us. It could mean I want to be a little closer."

"You want to be closer to Baldy?"

He laughed and Melanie felt a genuine smile forming on her lips.

"I like you, Melanie Fiske. You make me laugh. I haven't done enough of that lately. I'll see you around."

"You'll see me tomorrow when you stop by for me to check those stitches."

He touched his forehead in a salute. His gaze shot past her head and his grin faded as Silas opened the infirmary door behind her. There seemed to be a definite purpose when Tom reached out to catch the end of her braid and give it a little tug. "I'll stop by in the morning, Doc, and give you that first defense lesson."

"See you then." Melanie followed Tom out into the stifling heat, standing on the porch and watching him stride down the gravel road toward the parking lot. She squatted to pull the dead heads off her geraniums, hoping Silas would get the hint to leave.

He didn't.

Silas joined her on the porch before she'd pruned her way to the third plant. "You're getting mighty cozy with the new guy."

She shrugged off the accusation in his tone. "We were having a conversation."

He clamped his hand like a vise around her upper arm and pulled her to her feet, spilling the wilted flowers from her fingers. "Make sure that's all you have. If Roy gets Deanna knocked up before she gives my proposal the attention it deserves, I'm coming for you. Your uncle promised I'd inherit. That means marrying one of you."

She jerked her arm from his grasp. "Plead your case with Deanna."

She knelt to pick up the mess of flowers on her front walk.

But Silas couldn't stand hearing sass from a woman. "You don't want to cross me, Mel. Henry said you needed to be getting married and making babies. I'm your best choice here."

There was a whole wide world out there, bigger

than the virtual prison of these 500 acres. If this bully was the best she could do… If she had to lie with him and bear his child… Melanie pushed to her feet. "You don't love me. I don't even think you like me. How could you ever possibly be happy with me?"

"Because your last name is Fiske."

"That's insulting. I'm a person. I have feelings. If you stop to think, so do you."

He turned away to spit into the grass. "Deanna thinks I'm too old for her."

So the big brute was capable of an emotion beyond greed and anger. "If your sales pitch to her wasn't any better than the one you just gave me, it's no wonder she won't give you the time of day. Neither will I."

"It's not like men are knockin' down your door to get to you. Henry is going to make you marry someone to keep you here, and it might as well be me."

"Never. Going. To happen." She was on a roll today—pushing limits, asking questions, getting herself into trouble. Why not poke the bear one more time? She tipped her gaze to Silas's black eye. "Have you heard anything more about Richard? Any idea where he is? SueAnn doesn't need to be stressing about her brother's disappearance right now."

Silas might have a temper, but he was no fool. He wouldn't be riled into admitting anything. "I'm more interested in what you were doing out at your daddy's boat."

"I was swimming."

"You're lying."

But Melanie wouldn't be taunted into revealing anything, either. "Richard was sober when he left. He was cleaning up his act for SueAnn's sake. He wanted to be a good role model for his niece or nephew." She took a step toward Silas and dared him to tell her the truth. "Do you know where Henry sent him to work? Do you know if Sheriff Cobb arrested him? Was there an accident?"

"Why are you asking me?"

"You keep telling everyone you're in charge of things around here."

"I don't keep track of hard cases like Richard once they leave the farm."

She backed him right off the edge of her porch. "I think *you're* lying. I think you *do* know something."

He raised his hand and Melanie flinched. "You watch your tone with me, girl."

The door opened behind her and Daryl came out. Silas lowered his hand as her friend moved up beside her. "SueAnn's taking a nap. We can talk now."

Silas pointed a thick finger at her. "This conversation isn't over."

Which part? Refusing to tell her what he knew about Richard? Or *threatening* to marry her?

Feeling sick to her stomach from the stress of yet another confrontation, Melanie watched the two men head toward the main house. She walked around the side of her cottage and tossed the dead flowers in the compost bin. She winced as she lowered the lid and pushed up her sleeve to see the clear imprint of Silas's hand on her arm.

She hadn't grown up in a world filled with threats like this. Or maybe she had, and she'd been too naive, too consumed with loneliness and unfulfilled wishes to notice it around her. But she was aware now. She was aware of the violence and secrets, the missing friends and the lies.

She was aware of being watched. Right now.

Inhaling the smell of the fetid compost as she steeled her resolve, Melanie turned to see Tom Maynard, standing at the open door of his black pickup, watching her. Even from this distance, she could read the grim look on his face.

The man who'd no doubt witnessed that entire interchange with Silas wasn't the distracting Tom with the crooked grin and familiar hands. He wasn't even the friendly Tom with ties to Kansas City. That was scary-soldier Tom. The man who wore a gun and a knife and made her think she'd finally met someone besides herself willing to stand up to Henry and Silas.

He scraped his palm over his spiky hair and gave her a curt nod before locking up his truck and strolling across the gravel road to meet up with Silas and Daryl.

Why was Tom so fascinated with her?

And why did it unsettle her so much that he was?

Chapter Six

"Thanks." Melanie took the icy glass of lemonade from Deanna and scooted over on the porch railing at Henry and Abby's house to make room for the younger woman while they enjoyed the view of the men loading a truck in the parking lot. Now that the fishing dock and shops were closed for the day, they could relax. "I can use a cold drink."

"Not a problem." Deanna swung one long leg over the railing and then the other. Melanie buried her smile behind a long swallow of the cooling liquid. Deanna was risking splinters in her backside wearing denim cutoffs that short. But the daring change of clothing paid off. Roy Cassmeyer tripped with the crate he was carrying and stumbled into the loading dock on the back of the truck because his eyes had been glued on Deanna's legs instead of his destination. "What is the temperature out here this evening? A hundred?"

"At least." Maybe a little hotter from Roy's point of view. Melanie had to take another drink of the tart liquid to hide her amusement.

Melanie appreciated the shade as much as the raised perspective on the Jackson Trucking semi parked in front of the bakery and craft shop. Phyllis Schultz was checking off a manifest on a clipboard while the potbellied driver chowed down on a slice of pie beside her. Phyllis and her friend Bernie Jackson, however, weren't the scenery Melanie was watching from her perch. Her eyes had latched on to the men moving furniture and boxes of trinkets made by the craftsmen on the farm from the shop into the back of the truck for distribution to outlets in Falls City, Warsaw and other small towns around the lakes. Truth be told, she was watching one man, in particular.

With a square of white gauze and tape sticking out like a tattoo against his tanned skin, Tom was easy to spot. With Silas off on an errand for her uncle, Tom was easily the biggest man here. Although she couldn't hear the words, she read the teasing remark he aimed at Roy's klutzy maneuver, and heard the resulting laughter among all the men.

Tom had a clever sense of humor that had tempted her to smile on more than one occasion. How unfair was it that someone so ruggedly built could also tell her an adorable story about being a toddler who'd stripped off all his clothes on an outing with his mother to go skinny-dipping in one of the fountains on the Plaza in Kansas City? Although it was impossible to ignore that body, which was fit enough to handle the farm's physical workload—and strong enough to make a believer out of her when he'd shown her how to break a man's nose or strangle him with his own shirt if she needed to defend herself—it was that sense of humor he shared in their morning meetings at the infirmary that spoke to something inside her. Tom seemed to have made more friends around the farm the past few days than she'd made in the past year. Strange for a man who preferred the solitude of the night shift.

After dinner, it had been all available hands on deck to help Bernie Jackson unload boxes of groceries and paper goods from the back of his truck and get them into Phyllis's walk-in pantry inside the bakery before any of the food supplies were tainted by the heat. Now speed had given way to muscle as the men loaded the craft pieces into the truck for transport.

"He's hot." Deanna must be equally mesmerized by the show of testosterone.

"I bet they all are."

Deanna peeked over the top of her sunglasses, rolling her eyes at the joke. Then she pushed the frames onto the bridge of her nose and turned her gaze back to the men. Most of them had taken off their shirts in deference to the heat. All of them were glistening with sweat. "I'm talking about the new guy."

Melanie was surprised at the resentment that soured the lemonade on her tongue. She looked forward to Tom visiting her cottage for a check of his injury, then sharing coffee and some conversation about KC. She'd even had a few naughty fantasies about turning the impersonal contact they shared when he gave her those self-defense lessons into something very personal.

But that didn't mean she had a monopoly on his company. She'd given him directions to a quiet spot at the lake, and he'd promised to help her and Daryl keep an eye on SueAnn. Those were the kinds of things friends did. The way he touched her hair or brushed against her just meant the man had no sense of boundaries—not that he was interested in her.

She had no claim on Tom, but if Deanna set her sights on him, then Melanie would have no chance at all to lure him over to the dowdy-cousin side. Not that she really wanted to get attached to any man here. Her plans to learn all she could about her father's death and then leave depended on her ability to stay unattached. Still, she heard a jealous voice inside her, and pointed out, "I thought you were into Roy right now."

"He's got muscles that Roy doesn't. Plus, he's got that whole bad-boy vibe going for him."

"Silas has that same bad-boy vibe," Melanie said. "And he wants to be with you."

Deanna dismissed Silas's obsession with a toss of her dark hair. "Do you suppose Duff dances?"

"How would I know?" With a stab of something that felt like an impending sense of loss, Melanie's gaze zeroed in on Tom's broad back as he hefted one end of a dining room table onto the truck. He released the table and turned to her. Even at this distance she could see his gaze narrowing, as if he knew she'd been staring at him and was wondering why. Melanie swung her legs back over the railing to face the house instead of those curious green eyes. Even with the cold drink, she could feel her temperature rising. This conversation was getting under her skin a lot more than it should have. "You call him Duff?"

"All his friends do."

Was Deanna simply repeating the party line Tom made with every introduction? Or had her cousin already gotten extra friendly with him? After working here for a week, was Melanie the only person still calling him Tom?

"I wonder if he's going to the Lake Hanover dance. I think I'll ask him." Deanna looked over at her and laughed. "Relax, Mel. I'm not making plans to steal your man."

"He's not my man."

"I bet he could be if you tried. He's really into you for some reason. But you know, there's such a thing as playing *too* hard to get. If you need some makeup tips, or want to borrow some clothes or— Oh, wait. Nothing I have would fit you, would it?" Her frown transformed into an excited smile. "We could go shopping in Falls City. I wonder if Duff would prefer you in a dress or tight-fitting jeans."

"Stop trying to be helpful," Melanie muttered.

When the front door swung open, she nearly leaped to her feet at the chance to escape the unsettling conversation. "Aunt Abby."

"Girls?" Her aunt peeked out the screen door. With her hair drawn back into a ponytail, Abby was clearly in cleaning and planning mode. "If you've had enough of a break, I could use your help. I need to get the decorations for the dance down from the attic. Since we're hosting it this year, I want everything to look just right."

"I'll go." Melanie handed her lemonade glass off to her aunt and went inside. She'd have volunteered to scrub the toilets if it meant getting away from Deanna's *helpful* observations about Melanie's shortcomings when it came to getting a man to notice her. But her mood shifted from thoughts of escape to the opportunity to do more exploring to see if she could find anything else that had belonged to her father. "What am I looking for?"

"Three boxes marked Independence Day," Abby called after her as Melanie hurried up the stairs. "I know it's past the Fourth, but I thought the red, white and blue would make colorful decorations around the barn. The boxes should be on the metal shelves."

"I'll find them." Abby turned her attention to Deanna while Melanie went to the end of the hallway and tugged on the rope to lower the attic stairs.

The air on the house's third floor was heavy and warm. Melanie picked up one of the flashlights stored on a shelf beside the opening in the floor and switched it on. When her beam of light bounced off the window in the back wall, she briefly considered opening it to get some sort of breeze. But if she was up here long enough to need a breeze to cool off, someone would surely start to question her disappearance and come looking for her.

She'd have to settle for quick rather than thorough when it came to her search for clues. Melanie spotted the boxes as soon as she pulled the string to turn on the bare lightbulb overhead. She carried them to the top of the steps one by one, using each trip to study the shelves, furniture and hanging storage bags to see if she spotted anything that reminded her of her father.

The box where she'd found the watch seemed to have conveniently disappeared, but she read every label, hoping something would draw her attention. Halloween. Deanna—High School. Rodeo Pageants. Melanie lifted the lid on that box and found several mementos from her aunt's career as a beauty queen. Although her winning crown and hat were displayed in a hutch downstairs, this box contained framed certificates from county-fair contests, along with a couple of photograph albums and some of the decorative tack Abby had used when she'd competed.

Something about the carved grommets that had once decorated a show saddle, and the pockmarked chain of a bridle with the bit still attached, reminded Melanie of the ring of black steel she'd found out on her father's boat. She tucked the flashlight beneath her chin and dug into her jeans to pull out the ring, holding both it and the chain up to the light. Not that the ring matched in terms of age or style, but the shape was similar. With the oblong protrusion on one side of the ring, and a tiny hole like the eye of a needle in the middle of that protrusion, it could be a link in some other type of chain.

If so, how did that help her? What would a chain be doing on her father's boat? The metal was new, and the boat hadn't been seaworthy for some time. This odd-shaped ring probably wasn't a link to anything. Why couldn't she just find a box marked Leroy Fiske or Don't Show This to Mel? Ending up with more questions than answers, Melanie dropped the chain inside the box and pushed it to the back of the shelf to pull the next one forward.

Pulling the flashlight from beneath her chin, she shined the light into the space vacated by the box. "What is that?"

Gauging the length of time she'd been up in the attic by the perspiration trickling into the cleft between her breasts, Melanie decided to risk a few more minutes of explore time. She twisted her hair into a rope and tucked it inside the collar of her T-shirt. It wasn't the box or the empty space that had snagged her curiosity, but what lay behind it.

A door.

A locked door, to be precise.

She pulled a couple of boxes to the floor to lighten the weight of the shelf, then lifted one corner slightly and angled it away from the wall. She froze for a second at the screech of metal across the wood floor. But there was no thunder of running feet at the noise, no shouts of alarm from below. With only the sound of her own excited breathing to keep her company, she continued her search. Melanie sidled behind the shelf to inspect the door that was barely as tall as she. She ran her fingers across the shiny steel hasp and padlock that sealed the door shut, wondering at the purpose of a new lock on an old door and who held the key to open it.

"What are you hiding in here?" And who was hiding it?

She tugged on the padlock, just in case the old door frame was brittle enough to break away, but the wood held fast. She needed a pry bar or a pair of bolt cutters to get inside.

Or a chain.

The fear of discovery hurried her feet around the shelves. She opened the box of Abby's souvenirs and grabbed the broken bridle chain. With a little seesawing, the links were narrow enough that she could slip the chain behind the hasp just where the door and frame met. She scratched some of the wood pulling it through. But if she could get a long enough length on either side, she could wind the ends around both hands and pull, hopefully forcing the screws to pop. Just a little...

A board creaked in the shadows behind her.

Melanie spun around. She was still alone up here, right?

Then she heard another creak. And another.

"Oh, damn." Someone was coming up the attic steps.

She tugged the chain from behind the hasp and hurriedly lifted and shoved the metal shelves back into place. There was no way to mask the noise, so she didn't bother shutting off the lights and hiding. But if she was quick, she wouldn't really have to lie about what she was doing up here. She thrust one box onto the shelf and picked up the other.

She froze a second time when a beam of light hit her back, silhouetting her head and shoulders against the box she hadn't quite slid back into its place.

"What are you doing up here, girl?" Henry's voice sounded more curious than perturbed. But all that would change if he suspected she'd been snooping around the door that someone had gone to a great deal of trouble to camouflage to keep inquisitive people like her away.

And then she realized she still held the chain in her hand. There was no way she could return it to the proper box without giving away that she had taken it. Pulling up the hem of her T-shirt, she stuffed it into the front of her jeans as quietly as she could before turning away from the box and praying she'd pushed it far enough onto the shelf so that it wouldn't crash to the floor behind her.

Melanie pointed her flashlight back at Henry, blinding him a bit to the mess she'd left behind her. "Aunt Abby asked me to get the boxes of decorations for Saturday's barn dance."

Henry dropped the beam of his flashlight to the boxes she'd set at the top of the steps. "Looks like you got 'em all right here."

"I didn't remember how many there were. I wanted to make sure." Melanie used the moment out of the spotlight to take several steps across the attic before Henry captured her in the beam of his light again. She pasted a smile on her face and shrugged.

"It's hotter than blazes up here and I don't want to have to make another trip."

His brown eyes were unreadable orbs in the attic's dim light. "You sure you weren't pokin' your nose into things that don't belong to you?"

"This used to be my home, too." Melanie moved her arm over the bulging coil of chain tucked beneath her clothes. Hopefully, there were enough shadows in the room to mask the bulge of the contraband she'd been forced to take. "Anyway, could you blame me? I miss Dad. I miss the way things used to be when I was little and he and I were a family. I even miss the two of you being silly together—fishing together for hours and telling stories." She glanced around the rafters and walls, carefully avoiding the shelves and hidden door behind her. "You've saved things from Deanna's life and Abby's and yours—but not Dad's. Or mine."

Melanie curled her toes into her boots, forcing herself to stand fast as her uncle closed the distance between them.

"I miss Leroy, too. I don't have much left of him besides memories—and you. Once you could walk, you almost always tagged along with us." He surprised her by squeezing her shoulder. She couldn't help a tiny flinch, but she refused to give away the depth of her suspicions by running from him. "I'll never forgive myself for not standing up to the great-aunts and cousins who helped themselves to the baby quilt our mother made for you before she died. They took Grandpa's rolltop desk and all of Leroy's fishing lures he tied, and who knows what else that should have gone to you. I guess they sold them as collectibles and antiques. Your daddy left the land to me, and I've provided well for you, I think—but the rest of it should have gone to you. I'm sorry I can't change the past."

"So am I."

Henry pulled away to hook his thumb into the strap of his overalls, no doubt hearing the cynicism coloring her tone. "I was a grieving man. I had a baby of my own and a new little girl thrown into my lap who kept askin' for her daddy. If it wasn't for Abby and her strength, I don't know how I would have gotten through that time."

Melanie turned her head and blinked, hating the unshed tears that made her eyes gritty. She wanted to feel anger, not sadness. Crying wouldn't answer any questions about her father's death. "Maybe because his body was never recovered, I feel like I have nothing of his except that old wreck of a boat."

"Tell you what, I'll make some calls—see if any of those surviving relatives still have something of Leroy's. If they aren't willing to share, I'll offer to buy it for you." Didn't he look pleased with himself? Almost like he cared about her. "I'll make it an early birthday present."

But what kind of man lied to his niece, the woman he'd supposedly raised as his own daughter, and smiled about it? It was a lot easier to feel the anger now.

"What about Dad's pocket watch?" The heavy

gold circle burned against her skin inside her pocket. "I remember him carrying it every day—showing it to me nearly every night. I'd love to have that back."

Henry scratched at one of his sideburns, frowning as if she'd spoken gibberish. "You asked me about that before. I told you it's probably at the bottom of the lake with him."

Liar!

Instead of giving her anger a voice or daring him to lie about the hidden door, as well, Melanie opted for escape. She returned her flashlight to its shelf and picked up a box. "I'd better get these down to Abby."

"I'll give you a hand."

Did she imagine he hesitated at the top of the stairs? She could hardly turn back to see if he was shining his light around the attic, checking to see if she'd found anything she shouldn't have.

Depositing the box in the kitchen where Deanna and Abby were working, she answered her aunt's thanks with a muttered "Sure."

"Melanie." She paused in the doorway at her aunt's voice and smelled the spice of her perfume coming closer. "Deanna tells me you need to go into town to shop for a dress for the dance." Great. Abby and Deanna had been making plans for her love life again. But as Melanie faced her aunt, the bridle chain shifted inside her jeans and started to slide down her pant leg. "We'll be going into Falls City on Thursday. You're welcome to come with us."

Melanie angled her hips to one side and hooked one ankle behind the other to keep the chain from sliding out onto the floor. If her hidden treasure was discovered, explaining why she had the weird souvenir would be awkward at best. At worst, it would make access to the attic to get a look behind that locked door impossible. So, instead of grabbing her pants and running, she stood there in a silly pose and hoped this conversation would end quickly. "I really have to go to this dance?"

"It would be an insult to Henry if you didn't. He's paying for everything. The festival is our last big celebration before harvest. I won't let you wear boots and an old T-shirt to a party." Melanie pressed her hand against her thigh as Abby moved closer to pull Mel's hair out of her T-shirt. "Maybe we can do something with this mess while we're in town, too."

Melanie nodded, backing toward the hallway. She backed right into Henry and nearly knocked the two boxes he carried from his hands. "Sorry."

"Why are you in such a rush?" he asked. "Did our conversation upstairs upset you?"

"What conversation is that?" Abby asked.

A quick escape was no longer an option.

Henry set the boxes on the kitchen table. "She asked me about Leroy again, where some of his things might have gotten to over the years."

"Is that so?" Abby's dark eyes were suddenly a lot less indulgent. "I told you that's a sore subject for your uncle."

"And it's not for me?" Melanie snapped. "I have a right to ask questions. He was my father. I want to know how he died. I want to know *why* he died."

"It happened fourteen years ago," Henry reminded her.

She swung around to vent her frustration on him, too. "And I still don't know anything about that night. Why would he go out so late? Was he meeting somebody? If strange things are happening around this place now, why couldn't they have happened fourteen years ago, too?"

"Strange things?" Abby took a step toward her. "What strange things are you talking about?"

Henry put up his hand, silencing his wife. "Leroy used to tell me all his plans. How he was going to turn the lake into a recreational area and give guided fishing tours to city folks who wanted to enjoy a bit of country living on the weekends. I saw the plans for the new house he'd wanted to build for Edwina, but after her death, he decided to stay in this house that Grandpa built. He told me a lot of things over the years. But not where he was going the night he died." Henry wasn't a tall man, but he was tall enough to force Melanie to tilt her chin to hold his gaze when he moved closer. "This is *my* home now. I built this farm and business and everything you see into the success we all enjoy. I gave you your own place. I sent you to school. I did everything a father would do for his child."

"You're not my father."

"I will not be talked to like this, like you think I know something about your daddy's death, like there was something unnatural about it, in my own home."

Melanie's pulse hammered in her ears as the rage swelled inside her.

Abby could probably read the heat crawling up Melanie's neck. "Maybe you'd better go back to your cottage, Mel, until your temper cools off."

"Maybe I'd better." And then she was pushing past Henry and hurrying out the front door...where she came face-to-face with Silas. Or rather, face-to-chest—with the strap of a rifle that hung across his back. And the man was wearing black leather gloves. In this heat wave? Talk about strange things. "Where have you been all day?" she snapped. "The rest of us emptied and loaded that entire truck without you. I thought a good man was supposed to lead by example."

Silas gripped the strap in one gloved hand and a thick manila envelope in the other down by his side. He didn't budge. He didn't have the courtesy to speak directly to her, either. "What's eatin' her?" he asked her uncle.

Melanie was summarily dismissed, without any answers, without any kind words.

She felt Henry's heat at her back. But he wasn't there to defend her or offer any explanation for her red-faced exit. "Is that the package I asked for?"

"Yes, sir." Silas held up the envelope. "Should I go ahead and give it to Mrs. Fiske?"

"She may be in charge of the books, but I'm the boss." Henry reached around Melanie for the envelope. "You go on in the house and have a glass of lemonade in the kitchen while I take care of some business in my office."

"Be happy to, sir."

Melanie had to step aside for Silas to enter. She kept right on moving, across the porch and down the stairs. Grabbing the snakelike chain winding its way down her pant leg, she ran across the yard, across the gravel road, up the sidewalk and into her house, slamming the door behind her.

Her steps carried her all the way to her kitchen table, where she braced her fists against the top and let out a feral groan of pure, pent-up emotion.

The rawness of tears and frustration burned her throat when the door opened and closed behind her again. A deep voice asked, "What's wrong?"

Chapter Seven

Melanie spun around and charged at Tom Maynard. "Get out of here! This is my home. There should be at least one place on this farm where I can have some privacy."

He caught her wrists when she tried to push him toward the door. "Hey. I'm not the enemy here."

"Let go!" She tried one of those crazy extrication moves he'd taught her, twisting within his grasp.

But he countered with a move he hadn't taught her, and the next thing she knew, he'd cupped her jaw between his hands and tilted her face to catch her tear-blurred gaze. "Talk to me, Doc. You bolted across that compound. What happened?"

She blinked until she saw concern and maybe the hint of anger in the hard line of his eyes.

"Melanie?" The soft growl of her name was her undoing. Fisting her hands into the damp cotton of his shirt, she walked into his chest, tucking her head beneath his chin and burrowing against his strength and heat. His arms went around her, anchoring her to him. He slipped his palm along the nape of her neck, lifting the weight of her hair off her back as he dipped his lips against her ear. "Did Silas threaten you again? You need to talk to me. At least tell me you're not hurt."

"I'm not hurt," she whispered between sobs. She flattened her palms against his chest and made a token effort to smooth out the wrinkles she'd put in his black T-shirt. But she couldn't quite bring herself to put any distance between them. "I'm sorry. I know I didn't ask..."

"You hold on as hard as you need to."

Melanie debated for all of three seconds before sliding her arms around Tom's waist. His shoulders folded around her like a shield. Hold on, she did. She dug her fingertips into the corded muscles of his back, and all those months of suspicion and lies and confronting the past on her own came pouring out with an embarrassing outburst of tears. She turned her ear to the strong beat of Tom's heart, focused her thoughts on the tender stroke of his hands on her neck and back, absorbed the heat of his body into the chilly isolation of her life.

The man had no qualms about touching and butting into her business, and right now she needed someone who wasn't afraid to crash through the protective walls she'd erected around her heart. Melanie couldn't remember the last time she'd been held like this, the last time she'd felt safe enough to cry. She couldn't remember the murmur of soothing little nonsense words or leaning against someone else's strength. She couldn't remember someone caring.

They stood like that for several minutes. Tom didn't budge, didn't retreat, didn't let go until the worst of the flood had passed and she sagged against him.

"You okay, Doc?"

Gradually, she became aware of the musky spice of his skin. She realized those tree-trunk thighs and solid chest created an enticing friction against her softer curves. She freely admitted—to herself— that she was far more attracted to her new friend than any mere friend should be. But Melanie didn't want to risk alienating the one man she was beginning to trust. She'd already bawled her eyes out in front of him and left a damp spot on the front of his shirt. Telling him that the prickly, plain-Jane virgin of the Fiske Family Farm was developing feelings for him would probably send him running for cover, and she'd be alone again. In control of her thoughts now, she sniffled into his shirt and eased her death grip on him. "I'm okay now. But if you tell anyone I was crying…"

He leaned back against her arms still anchored at his waist but made no other effort to disengage from the embrace she'd forced upon him. He seemed oddly content to brush the long red waves away from her face, gently coming back to catch the strands that stuck to her moist cheeks. A crooked grin cut through the stubble that shaded his jaw. "I thought you didn't like secrets, Doc."

"Tom…" She started to protest the nickname she hadn't earned, but he wouldn't hear it.

"This secret's safe with me." He finally broke the contact between them and crossed his finger over his heart. "I promise. You are smart, funny and do not cry if anyone asks me."

"I'll hold you to that." Smiling with him eased the embarrassment of shaking her left leg and finally allowing the bridle chain to tumble out of her jeans into a pile on the floor. She didn't care how odd it must look. She picked up the chain and twisted it into a coil before setting it on the denim place mat at her kitchen table. Thirsty and hot after that crying jag, she headed to the sink to run herself a glass of water. She drank half of it and poured the rest of it over her hands to splash against her face and neck. "I'm not normally a crying type of woman. Hope I didn't embarrass you."

"I never mind the opportunity to put my hands on you," he teased.

Melanie felt her skin coloring with heat, but this blush was a pleasant sort of warmth compared to the feelings that had overwhelmed her a few minutes earlier. "You're relentless."

"I am," he admitted in a tone that was as refreshingly honest as it was unapologetically masculine. Tom crossed to the table to pick up the chain and identify it. "Did you steal this from Henry's house?"

"Didn't mean to." She dried her hands and dabbed her face with a towel. "But I didn't have a chance to put it back without being seen. Henry caught me snooping… Wait. Were you spying on me?"

"Were you worried about getting caught?" he

questioned without answering her query. "Is that why you were running like death was chasing you?"

Melanie shivered at his particular choice of words. "That's a creepy analogy to make."

"I call things as I see them." He dropped the chain back onto the table. "I thought I sensed a look of distress when you were on the porch with Deanna. When we were done with the truck I wanted to catch up with you and see what was going on. What did the Barbie doll say that upset you?"

Melanie shook her head, unwilling to admit how her cousin's interest in Tom had gotten under her skin. "Deanna thinks you're hot. She's hoping you'll ask her to the dance on Saturday."

"And that upset you enough to steal a piece of horse tack from your uncle's house?" He came over to the sink where she stood and leaned his hip against the counter beside her. "Should I be flattered?"

This time, she couldn't help but smile at his teasing. "All right. So maybe I was a little jealous. Can't I have at least one friend here? Does she really need to have every man on the place drooling after her?"

"One, I don't drool for any woman. Two, I'm not interested in someone who doesn't get my jokes. And three…" He reached out and palmed the side of her hip, drawing her half a step closer. "I like some curves I can get my hands on."

"You like…?" The sensation of his firm grip branding her through her jeans stole her breath. Her blood raced with unexpected anticipation to the naughty parts of her, and she found herself hoping he'd do something more to excite, er, ease the heavy feeling in her breasts and the needy constriction of muscles between her thighs. She just needed a friend to talk to right now. She shouldn't be wishing he'd pull her even closer, right? She pushed away and put some space between them before her brain completely short-circuited. "That's not why I was running. I can deal with Deanna. Henry and Abby and Silas—they all upset me."

"Should I tell you that you're blushing again?"

"No." The heat crawling up her neck intensified.

"Well, I will tell you that I *am* flattered to hear you were a little jealous. I have no interest in your cousin, and I don't like the idea of anyone upsetting you." His amusement ended with his fingers sifting through the hair at her temple, tucking the waves behind her ear and smoothing the length of it behind her shoulder. "Now tell me what happened."

She explained her suspicions about her father's so-called accident. She told him about the door she'd found in the attic and her father's watch. With big, bad Tom Maynard staring down at her, his arms folded across his chest and his probing green eyes watching the nuances of her expression, Melanie told him everything that had happened fourteen years ago and the mysterious things that seemed to be happening around the farm now.

"And you think Henry, Abby and Silas know more about what happened to your father than they're letting on?"

"Yes. But they won't talk about it so I have to

snoop around my own family to find answers for myself. Do you know there's no sheriff's report on Dad's
drowning? At least nothing in Sheriff Cobb's files."
When she didn't think she could stand that green-
eyed scrutiny anymore, Melanie opened the refrigerator door. "You want something cold to drink?"

"I'll take one of those beers."

She opened two and carried them to the table. "I
probably shouldn't be telling you any of this. I don't
know who to trust anymore. They insult me or lie
to me or just tick me off."

"Now who's the antisocial one?" Tom clinked the
neck of his beer bottle to hers.

Melanie took a swallow of the bitter brew, savoring the chill running down her throat. "The more I
push for answers, the more I get stonewalled. It's not
like I can go to the authorities with my suspicions.
Sterling Cobb is Henry's best friend. And the sheriff before him was as corrupt as—"

"Wait." Tom glanced over his shoulder.

"—they come. Supposedly, all his records disappeared before Sterling was elected."

"Melanie—"

"Who knows if he even investigated Dad's death
as anything other than…" Before she understood either his warning or his intent, he'd slipped his hand
behind her waist and pulled her hips into his. "What
are you—"

Tom dipped his head and pressed his lips against
hers, stopping up her words with a kiss. Her lips
parted with a surprised gasp and he angled his mouth

to capture her bottom lip between his and then tease the top lip with the raspy stroke of his tongue. When the startled moment passed, her hand came up to caress the rough angle of his jaw and guide his warm mouth back to the tentative foray of her own lips. She heard a low-pitched groan from deep in his throat that triggered an answering need inside her. His tongue darted into her mouth to dance against hers, giving her a taste of hops and heat that was more intoxicating than the beer itself.

Part of her was aware of his free hand sliding something into his pocket, but even that thought vanished when that hand cupped her bottom and lifted her onto her toes. As Tom's mouth moved over hers, Melanie slid her fingers around his neck, learning and loving the tickle of beard stubble against her palm. The tips of her breasts pinched with excitement at the friction of his harder chest rubbing against hers.

She heard the front door close with a firm click. "Am I interrupting?"

The room spun around her as Melanie dropped onto her heels and pushed away at Abby's teasing tone. But Tom's grip tightened around her waist, preventing her escape. What an idiot she was, giving in to a few compliments and this embarrassing visceral attraction she felt. But when she tipped her chin up to tell him exactly what she thought of a man who would play on her loneliness and inexperience, she discovered narrowed green eyes boring down into hers, warning her to do what? Hide her confusion? Not feel hurt? Play along?

Play along with what?

She'd been so caught up in the need to share her frustrations and fears with a willing ear that she'd missed the soft rapping at her front door. Now her aunt was waltzing into Mel's kitchen with a sympathetic smile and a basket of something that smelled fresh from the oven. "I knocked, but no one answered. I was worried about you, dear. I brought you some cookies Phyllis just baked."

The bridle chain!

Realizing her fingers were still clutched in the front of Tom's shirt, Melanie released her grip and scrambled away from him, scanning the tabletop in a panic. But the chain she'd taken from her aunt's souvenir box was nowhere to be seen.

Then she saw Tom pat the front pocket of his jeans. She glanced up to a barely discernible nod. He'd hidden it for her so her snooping wouldn't be discovered. But why the kiss?

Suspicion warred with gratitude inside her, but she couldn't very well confront him about his motives with Abby in the room. So she turned to her aunt. "They smell yummy," Melanie conceded, although right now she had no appetite. "Chocolate chip?"

"I know they're your favorite." Abby smiled at her. "Think of them as a peace offering. I'm sorry if our conversation upset you."

"Conversation?" Abby considered that argument

and cold dismissal a mere conversation? One that could be forgotten with a bribe of sugar and chocolate?

But with Tom's gaze tracking her every move, Melanie opted for a reply as sincere as she suspected her aunt's apology might be. "I'll get over it."

"Of course, you will." Abby set the basket on the table and unwrapped the red napkin inside to display the treats. "I see you've already found your own comfort. You two should share these." Abby stroked her fingers along Tom's forearm and winked. "Good work, Mr. Maynard. Our Melanie is a tough nut to crack. I'll see you both tomorrow."

Melanie nodded as her aunt sashayed out the door. It took her brain a few moments to switch gears from the surprise of Abby's visit to the surprise of Tom's kiss. She locked the door before she turned and leaned against it. "Good work? Pretending you're interested in me is *good work*?"

"If you don't want someone to know your secrets, then you need to stop talking. I heard her lurking outside and thought someone might be listening. That's not why I kissed you." When he made a move toward her, she crossed to the coffee table to retrieve the book she'd been reading. "It's not the only reason I kissed you."

"Save the sweet talk, *Duff*." She hugged the book to her chest, sending a clear message to keep his distance as she carried the book to the table. "And you wonder why I don't trust men coming on to me. I thought it was okay for me to…"

"I was very okay with it."

Despite the husky approval in his tone, she plopped the book down in front of her as her humiliation bubbled up into a temper. "I must be really entertaining for you to play with. You're no better than Silas. I'm just a means to an end. For whatever it is you're up to."

"Don't you dare lump me in with that jackass." Tom splayed his fingers at his waist, creating a formidable profile. "Yes, I kissed you because I didn't think you wanted anyone to hear the chat we were having. I was looking out for you."

"You couldn't tell me to shut up?"

"And have you argue with me?" He pulled the chain from his pocket and dropped it link by link onto the table. "How did you want to explain this to your aunt?"

"Fine. So I appreciate the save." Melanie gestured toward the door where her aunt had exited. "But now she thinks you and I are a thing."

"Is that so bad?" He shrugged, still trying to sell her on his sincerity. "Look, maybe you're blind, or maybe you're just ignoring it, but we've got some chemistry here. I'm not afraid to have your aunt sharing the news that we've got something going on. A rumor like that will help Silas keep his hands off you. It'll teach Deanna that not every man is into skinny, spoiled children. And it'll show these rubes around here that you've got backup."

Discouraging Silas from targeting her as a potential mate did have its appeal. And the notion of physical chemistry went a long way to explain these feelings she thought she had for Tom. But there had to be something in this for him. Plus, the fact that he, of all people—after she'd poured out her hurts and suspicions to him—was keeping secrets from her, too, grated against every nerve in her body. She picked up her beer and swallowed a cooling drink. "You think I need backup?"

"Everybody needs someone watching their back. Especially stubborn redheads who keep poking at mysteries no one wants to talk about." He circled the table, reaching out as if he wanted to touch her. "You've officially got me."

Melanie palmed the center of his chest and kept him at arm's length. "I suppose you expect me to have your back now, too?"

"I expect you to keep being my friend." He leaned into her hand, dropping his voice to a drowsy timbre. "But make no mistake, Melanie Fiske—I will be kissing you again. Things were just getting interesting when your aunt walked in."

Anticipation skittered through her veins at his matter-of-fact promise. Her fingertips curled into the soft cotton of his T-shirt. "Friends don't kiss each other like that."

"You don't want me to kiss you again?"

Her blush betrayed her before she could voice the proper protest. "You know I can't hide that I like you. Maybe because you're not one of them." She looked toward the door and the main house beyond. "Or maybe because you really talk to me and say what you think and…" She snatched away the fingers that were still clinging to the firm muscles of his chest and turned a pleading gaze up to him. "Just don't lie to me, okay? I want to be able to trust you."

"You can." Tom stepped back, his shoulders expanding with a deep breath. He crossed his arm over his chest and trailed his fingers over his healing shoulder. The hesitancy of the man who was normally confident made her think he was reconsidering that assurance. "Look, Doc, there's something I need to—"

"My name isn't Doc. I may never be a doctor, so you need to stop calling me that." She cut him off before he could feed her any more bunk that would make her regret this shaky alliance they were forming. She pulled out a chair to sit. "Let's just finish our beers."

"And our conversation." He pulled out the chair opposite her, swinging it around to straddle it. "You think your father was murdered and the previous sheriff wrote it off as an accident?"

"Maybe. If he even reported it." Melanie picked up a napkin to wipe away the condensation beading on the outside of her beer bottle, wishing she could clean up this mystery just as easily. "If there's nothing to hide, why won't anyone talk about it?"

"Would somebody around here have a motive to kill him?"

"Henry. Most of this land was left to Dad, with a smaller parcel for Henry to farm. When Dad passed, Henry got all of it."

Tom braced his elbows on the back of the chair and leaned forward, his eyes narrowing in that questioning gaze of his. "Your father didn't leave the farm to you? Or at least name a trustee until you reached a certain age?"

"There wasn't any will. There weren't any papers. None that Henry could find—or so he says. I had some greedy relatives who took everything of value. I didn't think I was ever going to have anything that was my father's until I found this." She pulled the watch from her pocket and handed it to Tom.

He read the engraving before opening the watch and looking inside. "This was your father's?"

"I found it in a box in Henry and Abby's attic. I know it's Dad's because of the engraving. The picture is my mother. You can't really tell anymore."

He studied the smeared portrait before snapping it shut and returning it to her. "Did you ask Henry about it?"

"Not directly. But I've asked him more than once if he had anything that belonged to Dad."

"And?"

"He denied it." Melanie rubbed her thumb across the engraving with loving reverence before sliding it back into her pocket.

"You think Henry knows where the will is? Or was? If someone is hiding a secret, it's probably been destroyed by now."

"Maybe it's hidden inside that closet."

He nodded at the possibility. "Anybody else with a motive to kill your dad?"

"Dad was a pretty quiet guy, but I think he was well liked. From an eleven-year-old's perspective, I thought he was perfect." She remembered the loss she and Tom shared and felt her heart squeeze with compassion. "You probably felt the same way about your mom. When you lose someone you love too soon, it's hard to remember any faults they might have had."

Tom nodded. "Mom was a beautiful, strong-willed woman. She had to be to raise all of us and be married to a cop. I suppose she could have rubbed somebody's feathers the wrong way. Broken another soldier's heart over in the UK before she married Dad and emigrated to the US. But you're right. Everybody I knew loved her."

"Your father is a cop?" He'd told her that the Kansas City police had arrested the men responsible for his mother's murder, but he'd never mentioned his father worked for KCPD. "Did he help with the investigation? He probably wasn't allowed to, I suppose. The son of a cop, hmm? I suppose that's why you're so good at asking all these questions."

Tom picked up his bottle, shifting in his seat before downing almost half of his beer. "Have you ever seen anything illegal go on around here?"

Another question. Maybe it was his way of deflecting any topic that got too close to that pain deep inside him. Melanie took another drink, trying not to think about tasting the beer on Tom's tongue when he'd kissed her. Answering his question seemed a lot easier than forgetting that kiss or ignoring the urge to comfort him.

"Firsthand? Fights like that one you got into that first day. No one ever presses charges. We have an occasional shoplifter. If the person returns the item, they let him go. If not, that's one crime Sheriff Cobb is willing to handle." She added, "We get the occasional hunter or fisherman who's on the property without a permit. But Silas turns them over to the Conservation Department."

"I don't mind the odd jobs I do around here. But patrolling the grounds around the farm and lake every night feels an awful lot like I'm part of a private security firm. Only, instead of working in a war zone, we're protecting citizens in our own backyard."

Melanie couldn't argue with that assessment. "Things are different than they were fourteen years ago. Having so many people around that no one seems to care when one of them goes missing? Not to begrudge you your job, but who hires ex-military for farmwork and tourism? Sometimes I think Henry's running some kind of militia group and he keeps me around because he's planning a war and he'll need a medic."

"A lot of money goes through this place," Tom suggested. "The Fiske Family Farm is more like Fiske City. Houses, cross streets, businesses, boat ramps and fishing docks? About the only thing you don't have here is a motel for guests."

Melanie pushed aside the basket of cookies and pulled the bridle chain closer to her. She pulled the watch and mysterious black ring out of her pocket, too, and made a small pile of clues that made no sense. "I'd leave tomorrow if I could. But I'm afraid I'll never find out the truth if I do."

Tom set his beer on the place mat in front of him and reached clear across the table to pick up the black metal ring. "What are you doing with a gas block?"

Melanie watched him turn the object over in his hand. "You know what that is?"

"It's part of a gun. Looks like a .750 ml gas block. For an AR-15 or some type of automatic rifle. It channels the gas from discharging the weapon back into the barrel of the gun to power the loading mechanism." He held it up between his thumb and forefinger and looked at her through the center hole. "Where's the rest of the rifle?"

Melanie snatched it from his fingers, preferring her speculation that it was a link from a chain to his certainty that it had come off a rifle. "I found it. Just this."

"Where? Can you show me?"

Soldier Tom was back, the intensity of his reaction to the object frightening her just a bit. "Why do you care?"

"If I'm going to do a decent job with security, I need to know who all owns a gun on this farm. I need to know who has the skills to take one apart and put it back together. I especially need to know if there's somebody out there in the woods running around with a customized assault rifle."

"Customized assault rifle?" Now he was really

FREE Merchandise is 'in the Cards' for you!

Dear Reader,

We're giving away FREE MERCHANDISE!

Seriously, we'd like to reward you for reading this novel by giving you **FREE MERCHANDISE** worth over $20 retail. And no purchase is necessary!

You see the Jack of Hearts sticker above? Paste that sticker in the box on the Free Merchandise Voucher inside. Return the Voucher today... and we'll send you Free Merchandise!

Thanks again for reading one of our novels—and enjoy your Free Merchandise with our compliments!

Pam Powers

Pam Powers

P.S. Look inside to see what Free Merchandise is **"in the cards"** for you!

W

e'd like to send you two free books like the one you are enjoying now. Your two books have a combined cover price of over $10 retail, but they are yours to keep absolutely FREE! We'll even send you 2 wonderful surprise gifts. You can't lose!

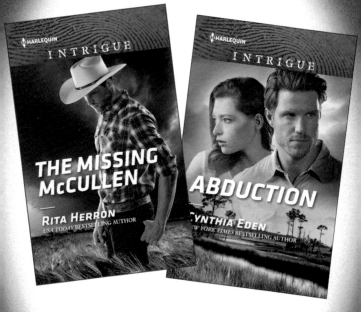

REMEMBER: Your Free Merchandise, consisting of **2 Free Books** and **2 Free Gifts**, is worth over $20 retail! No purchase is necessary, so please send for your Free Merchandise today.

Get TWO FREE GIFTS!
We'll also send you 2 wonderful FREE GIFTS (worth about $10 retail), in addition to your 2 Free books!

Visit us at:
www.ReaderService.com

scaring her. Silas had been wearing a gun like that when she'd seen him at the main house an hour ago. "It was on the *Edwina*. In a storage well. I didn't find any gun with it. Although…"

"What?" He was on his feet, striding around the table.

"Someone repaired the storage wells. The rest of the boat is falling apart, but the seals were watertight. Like someone was using them."

He pulled her to her feet. "I want to see that boat."

His suspicion blended with hers. "I can take you there tomorrow."

"Make it later tonight, when I head out for my security rounds." He brushed her hair off her forehead and tucked it behind her ear, easing the order into a request. "If you don't mind a late-night walk through the woods."

"I'll show you a shortcut," she offered. "Do you think it has something to do with my father?"

He shook his head. "That gas block is brand-new. It's the rest of the rifle that worries me, not knowing where it is or who owns it. I don't like surprises. It makes me think that I'm not the only thing out there in those woods at night who could kill someone."

Chapter Eight

Duff snapped the last picture of the *Edwina*'s storage wells with his phone. Since he was out of cell range here by Lake Hanover's northern shore, he'd transfer the photos over to his handler, Missouri Bureau of Investigation agent Matt Benton, when he met with him at the edge of the property later tonight.

The flash might have given away his location to anyone passing by, but that was the beauty of volunteering for Silas's night patrol. There were no passersby. Everyone on the farm had either turned in for the evening, or they'd gone into Falls City to spend their paycheck at one of the two bars in town.

A ripple of awareness pricked the short hairs at the nape of his neck. He *was* alone, right? He checked the tree line twenty yards away, and the wind-whipped surface of the lake beyond the weathered dock, to ensure no one was watching this detour from his usual route around the perimeter of the property. Judging by the fast-moving clouds blocking the moon overhead, a squall line was moving in—and any evidence he might be able to retrieve from the wreck Melanie had shown him last night would be washed away.

The electricity he felt must be a by-product of the coming storm. Still, it wouldn't do him any good to stop here longer than was necessary. Dismissing that sense of being watched, Duff pulled out a handful of swabs and plastic bags he'd filched from Melanie's infirmary and wiped the interior of each storage well. The chances of picking up trace amounts of gunpowder, metal fragments or packing residue that could prove weapons had once been stashed here were remote. But if there was any chance he could prove guns had been here, he was going to take it.

What other reason could there be to upgrade the storage bins on the beached boat? The dock wasn't one used by tourists coming in to fish, so there'd be little or no traffic in the area, making the *Edwina* a perfect place to hide the guns until it came time to ship them. The old gravel road leading to the lake was rutted and overgrown, but a truck with four-wheel drive—or an ATV like the one he was riding tonight—could get through to haul contraband. Maybe he'd just missed a delivery.

Or maybe Melanie's interest in her father's death had prompted Henry or Silas to move their stash before she discovered it. That meant locating other places to hide the weapons—like behind the locked door in the attic that Melanie had mentioned. Since he hadn't wormed his way into Fiske's inner circle yet, getting a look inside the main house would be a challenge. Maybe Melanie could get him in. Or maybe she'd be willing to go back up into the attic and get a picture of whatever was behind that door for him.

If he could bring himself to risk both her safety and revealing his identity.

As Duff sealed the swabs in plastic, his thoughts strayed to the farm's resident medic. It hadn't been an easy task to seduce Melanie over to his side. But he'd been more intrigued by the challenge of getting to know her than he'd been interested in any woman for a long time. She had a sense of humor he appreciated, a sharp brain inside her head, that amazing red hair and sweet, soft lips that seemed eager to be tutored by the right man.

He wanted to be that man. His body was warming up right now in anticipation of taking up where that kiss had left off, and the temperature had nothing to do with the heat brewing that storm overhead.

But that woman had a burr in her britches. She didn't trust anyone, and that stuck in his craw because he was the kind of guy a woman *should* believe in. She had that whole hang-up about men lying to her, and the fact he was in the middle of a colossal lie with this undercover assignment meant that whatever trust she was beginning to feel would fly out the window if she found out he was really Tom Watson, KCPD detective, and not Duff Maynard, ex-army sergeant.

That was the problem he should be stewing about, not whether or not he could make an opportunity to teach her a few more lessons in intimacy and seduc-

tion. She'd turned the tables on him last night, transforming a kiss meant to silence her into a real gut
kick of desire. Audience or not, he'd wanted to pull
her against him and plunder her willing mouth beneath his. For a few seconds, he'd forgotten that his
interest in her was supposed to be an act. Hell, he'd
damn near confessed that he was a cop when she'd
made not lying part of the deal to keep her talking
about everything she'd observed over the past few
months. Melanie had been hurting, and he'd hurt for
her. He understood her relentless need to find closure for her father's death—be it confirmation that
it was an unfortunate accident or proof of something
more sinister.

He wanted to do something to help her. Launch
an official investigation. Hold her if she needed another cry. Stand between her and anyone who dared
to upset her. He wanted to strip off the emotional
armor she wore like a Kevlar vest and show her just
how brave and beautiful she really was.

A gust of wind reminded him that he was here
to do a job, not to do Melanie Fiske. As much as his
gut was telling him the woman needed help in her
quest to expose the truth about her father's death, he
had to ignore this unexpected attraction and ease his
conscience by reminding himself that she'd needed
someone to listen to her last night, and he had. He
couldn't risk another mistake like the one he'd made
with Shayla by moving this relationship into something real. Listening would have to be enough.

Duff jumped off the boat before glancing up at

the lightning flashing through the clouds. Why did he feel Mother Nature was trying to warn him about something? He packed the swabs inside the saddlebag on the back of the ATV and paused for one more look around. He even took a couple of steps out onto the dock that rocked on the murky waves to make sure there wasn't someone on a boat in the cove.

Duff strode back to the ATV and climbed on. If there was someone out there watching him, he could explain his detour with the excuse that he'd heard or seen something and wanted to check it out. But spending too much time in any one place when he had miles to patrol would be harder to justify. The first drop of rain hit his cheek as he started the engine. He paused long enough to pull the green camo poncho from his saddlebag on over his head, checked to make sure he still had easy access to his gun beneath the poncho, then shifted into gear and rode into the woods, trying to beat the storm.

It was pouring by the time Duff reached the rendezvous point.

A black pickup was parked with its lights off on the overgrown service road by the fire tower that had been abandoned in the era of satellite technology. It wasn't noticeable unless someone knew to look for it. Duff shut off his ATV several yards back before approaching on foot.

The canopy of leaves and branches added another layer of shadows and secrecy to the site where he'd met Matt Benton four times in the past twelve days. Agent Benton's eyes must have adjusted to the darkness, because the truck door opened and he was pulling a black MBI ball cap on over his wheat-colored hair before Duff reached him.

The agent extended his hand to greet Duff. "Watson. You sure picked a hell of a night to hand over evidence for the lab. Everything all right?"

Duff nodded. Red-haired distractions aside, he was making progress on his investigation. "I confirmed that four handguns went out with a furniture shipment on Tuesday. All Glock 19s with the serial numbers sanded off. I marked one of them with an acid stain so we can track it. Nothing came in on the truck, though. Have you picked up any chatter from the bug I planted in Fiske's office?"

"The conversations are coming through loud and clear at our listening post, although we haven't heard of any deals being made. Unless Fiske is talking in code."

Duff had considered that possibility, too. "He mentioned tourists chartering boats for guided fishing tours. Any chance those could be when the hand-offs are being made?"

"Those shipments hit KC and St. Louis about once every other month. I'm guessing a new shipment will arrive shortly for distribution if it's not already here on the property."

Duff blinked away the moisture gathering on his eyelashes. "You got any other intel for me?"

Benton tucked the plastic bags Duff gave him inside the jacket he wore, and pulled out his phone in the same fluid motion. "I've got info on the names you gave me. Bernie Jackson's trucking business consists of two trucks—one driven by him, one by his brother-in-law. Everything looks legit, although it's Jackson's fifth try at starting his own company. Seems he's always hurting for money."

"Money troubles could be motive for helping Fiske and Danvers move the merchandise into the city."

"Maybe he's just a patsy and doesn't know what he's hauling for Fiske. We've got a forensic accountant looking into his records. I didn't want to raise a red flag, though, until we've got more from your end."

"My guess is they use multiple routes and storage areas, not just Jackson." Duff dried his fingers on his damp jeans before texting the pictures he'd taken of the *Edwina* to Benton's phone. "Did you find anything on that missing guy I texted you about?"

"Richard Lloyd?" Benton scrolled through the images on his phone to show Duff a couple of mug shots. "He's in the system for the drunk-and-disorderly arrests you mentioned, but no felonies. He hasn't popped up on legal warrants or traffic stops anywhere." Benton shook off the water dripping from the bill of his cap and showed Duff an image of a newspaper photo. "I thought this was interesting, though. From the *Falls City Weekly* a year ago. Could be coincidence. But it's not the kind I like."

The mix of thunder, wind and rain forced Duff to lean in so he could hear everything Matt was saying. He looked at the picture of Richard Lloyd,

decked out in head to toe camouflage gear, sitting on a tree stump holding up the antlers of the elk he'd shot. It wasn't the hunting prize that caught his attention, but the long wood stock of the Mauser rifle linked through the elbow of Lloyd's arm. Duff's blood boiled with the same anger he'd felt the day his grandfather had been shot. "The shooter at my sister's wedding used a Mauser." Did the fact that SueAnn's brother had gone missing have anything to do with the gun smuggling or the assault on the Watson family? "Can you blow up this picture and get a serial number off that rifle?"

Benton took his phone and returned it to his jacket. "The lab's working on it. If we can confirm it's an illegal firearm, and we can tie Lloyd to the Fiske Farm—"

"Then all I have to do is find him." SueAnn wouldn't be thrilled to learn her brother might be involved in the farm's illegal activities. But maybe it was time to talk to her and Daryl again to see what they could tell him about where Richard had gotten that rifle.

"You two done chatting about your investigation?" The passenger door opened on the truck and Duff's body tensed at the unexpected addition to their meeting. But his wariness rushed out with a smile as a tall, lanky man with dark brown hair climbed out, pushing his glasses up onto the bridge of his nose. "I assume time is of the essence here?"

"Niall?" Duff reached out to shake his brother's

hand before pulling his middle brother in for a back-slapping hug. "What are you doing here?"

"Agent Benton said you asked for a doctor. I volunteered. Which arm is it?"

"The task force physician checked me out a week ago—gave me a shot of antibiotics." Although he pulled up the edge of the poncho, Duff couldn't resist poking fun at his ME brother. "I don't know if I like the idea of someone who dissects dead bodies working on me."

As usual, his brainiac brother refused to take the bait. Niall pulled a penlight from his crime-lab jacket and lifted the bandage covering Duff's wound. He prodded the tender skin for all of ten seconds before covering the cut again. "No signs of infection. Whoever put the stitches in did good work. They're ready to come out, though."

Duff experienced a rush of pride at the compliment to her work that Melanie would never hear. "How are the wedding plans coming with you and Lucy? You haven't scared her off yet, have you?"

"We're still on track for September, and we'll be adopting Tommy right after. I'm assuming you'll be done with this case by then? Every Watson is involved in the ceremony now." There was no denying the smile that relaxed Niall's stern countenance whenever he mentioned the spunky little brunette and the baby who had captured his heart. "Dad agreed to walk Lucy down the aisle. I'm counting on you to be the best man."

"I'll be there." Duff understood that, despite all

their precautions, the longer the three of them were together, the greater chance they had of being discovered. But he was anxious to hear about his family. "How's Grandpa? I expect that's the real reason you're here."

"He's worried about you. Undercover is always a dangerous assignment. And once he heard you'd been in a knife fight…" Niall wiped the rain from his glasses before continuing. "I promised Dad and Grandpa I'd check on you personally. I'll give them a good report."

Duff had asked his brothers, sister and father, all members of KCPD in one aspect or another, to help as couriers while he was on this assignment—keeping him posted on Seamus Watson's recovery. "Is Grandpa getting any stronger?"

"His speech is showing a little improvement— Keir's fiancée, Kenna, has been working with him on that. But he's still not mobile like he used to be. Jane won't let Grandpa go anywhere without his walker." Jane was the live-in nurse their father had hired to take care of Seamus. "She doesn't want to risk him falling and reinjuring the muscles that are starting to regain strength. I know that's making him a little crazy."

"I imagine…"

Duff spun around at the soft squeak of water-logged boots.

"We've got company." Matt Benton was reaching for his gun.

But Duff had already spotted the red hair behind

the scrub cedars on the far side of the fire tower. He put his hand on the agent's arm, warning him to keep his weapon holstered, and turned to head off Melanie as she emerged from the trees. "Doc? What the hell are you doing here?"

"Why are they calling you Watson? This man's your brother and he's an agent? What's going on here?" She marched at them, her eyes shooting daggers with every streak of lightning that flashed through the sky. Her voice was a blend of hurt and accusation that cut straight through him. "I thought you wanted to be the only thing in these woods who could kill someone. Both those men are armed. You lied to me, Mr. *Watson*. That's the one thing I asked you not to do."

Duff turned to Matt and Niall before she reached them. "Go. I'll handle this."

Niall was reluctant to retreat. "Did we just blow your cover?"

He appreciated the show of support as much as he cursed his brother's refusal to do as he'd ordered. He pushed Niall toward the truck. "Go. Now. If she's out here, somebody else might be, too."

"Nobody followed me."

He ignored Melanie's reassurance. "Give my love to Grandpa. Tell him I'm gonna get the guy who hurt him." Matt Benton had already reached the truck. "Get me the answers I need."

Matt started the engine. "You're good?"

"I'm good." Duff turned to Melanie, assessing how much she'd seen and heard by the temper coloring her neck. Plenty, it seemed. He had to do some serious damage control or this case would go sideways fast. He was peripherally aware of Matt turning the truck around and driving off into the night. "We need to talk."

"Now you want to be straight with me?"

"We can't stay here." He peered into the shadows around them, wondering if anyone had followed Melanie as stealthily as she'd tracked him. "Are you alone?"

"Of course, I'm alone. I'm always alone."

Duff got the accusation. She'd let him into her life, had formed a tenuous relationship with him, and now she felt betrayed. This alliance was going down the tubes fast. "I never meant to hurt you. If you weren't so damn curious—"

"This is my fault? You're the liar." She crossed her arms in front of her. "I'm not moving until you tell me the truth."

"I have my reasons…" None of them seemed good enough to justify the pain that darkened her eyes. Her baby-oil scent was intensified by the rain that drenched her hair and clothes and left nothing to his imagination where it hugged her shoulders and breasts. "You're soaked to the skin." Duff pulled his poncho off over his head and tried to wrap it around her.

But she smacked the plastic to the ground. "I don't need a raincoat. Who were those men?"

"My brother, Niall, and Missouri Bureau of Investigation agent Matt Benton."

"Who are you?"

He wasn't lying his way out of this one. He wasn't about to walk away from this assignment because another woman had blown his cover, either. "Are you on foot?"

"I need a name. Not that I'm going to believe you."

Melanie was ready to verbally duke it out with him, but the argument couldn't happen here. He clamped his hand over her arm and walked her into the woods toward the ATV, tightening his grip when she tried to squiggle out of his grasp.

"Let go of me."

"We have to get out of here. I can't have this location compromised."

"Fine." She climbed onto the back of the ATV's wet seat, hugging her arms around her middle. Was that for warmth? Or a wall she was determined to resurrect between them? "Let's go someplace where we can have a private conversation. I think it's time you told me the truth."

Chapter Nine

"Be practical, Doc. I'm not the enemy here." The rain soaked through the shoulders of Duff's T-shirt, cooling his skin. Given her soggy state, Melanie had to be chilled to the bone. She fought him when he tried to give her his poncho a second time, but since he outweighed her by a good fifty pounds, he forced it over her head, anyway. "It's not much, but it'll warm you up."

"You're stalling, Mr. Maynard or Watson or whoever you are." She tugged her hair free of the hood. Its wet, heavy weight slapped against the back of the plastic poncho. "Let's go."

Duff climbed on in front of her and started the engine. "You'll have to hold on to me." She muttered something that wasn't very ladylike before her fingers curled around the sides of his waist. Her grip tightened when the ATV lurched forward, but he could feel the rain hitting his back as she held her body stiffly away from his. After traveling about half a mile to slightly smoother terrain, he slowed the four-wheeler and glanced back over his shoulder. He raised his voice over the noise of the engine. "You were at the lake, weren't you? How long have you been following me?"

"I saw you sneak away from the compound. I thought we could talk some more. About us." He felt a punch of guilt right in his gut. "There is no *us* happening, is there?" She sounded a little less angry, but the resignation he heard in her tone worried him. He'd never intended to hurt her. He'd never intended to care about hurting her. "Instead, I find you investigating Dad's boat without me and meeting with two men I've never seen before. You were using me to get closer to Henry."

"I don't care about your uncle right now. And I wasn't sneaking. I leave every night for my security patrol." He turned onto the path leading down to the old dock. "I've covered over five miles tonight. How did you find me?"

"I know all the shortcuts and hidey-holes around these hills. That fallen tree at the edge of the woods is hollow. I crawled into it while you were looking at the boat. Then I tracked the sound of the ATV. Once I knew you were heading north, I followed the creek bed. It's a straighter shot than the path you took." A streak of lightning lit up the sky, and he felt her jump at the answering clap of thunder. When she scooted a little closer, squeezing her thighs around his hips, he didn't mind. The physical connection between them seemed to be about the only way he could reach her. "Henry knows all the shortcuts, too, by the way."

That didn't bode well for maintaining his invisibility in these woods. "Does Silas?"

"Some. But I've known these hills years longer than he has. Plus, he's lazy. If he can't drive or ride his way to his destination, he sends someone else. He's not willing to cross Falls Creek, especially when it rains like this. Henry can barely get him onto the dock when they're loading or unloading the fishing boats."

"Sounds like he can't swim."

"Sounds like you're avoiding my questions." They hit a tree root that threw her against him, but she quickly scooted back to keep those few inches of distance between them. "Are you working for Henry? Buying off another cop like Sterling Cobb to cover up his secrets?"

Duff swiped the moisture off his face before steering the ATV toward the lake's edge. "I'm one of the good guys, Doc, even though, technically, I am a liar."

"At least you admit it."

"I'm part of a task force investigating the smuggling of illegal guns into Kansas City. We believe someone on your uncle's farm, if not Henry himself, is behind the gun trafficking."

She was silent long enough that he wondered if she'd heard him over the growl of the engine. But then she asked, "Guns? That's why you asked about the rifle part I found."

"That's why I was taking pictures of your dad's

boat. Those refitted storage wells are a perfect hiding place to stash weapons until they can be shipped out."

"You think the guns are coming through here?"

"I know they are. I loaded a box of handguns onto Bernie Jackson's truck. The box was sealed, but I'm nosy that way."

Instead of defending her uncle or the place where she'd grown up, he felt a heavy sigh against the back of his neck. "That would explain a lot. I thought the secrets all had to do with Dad. But if Henry's doing something illegal… No wonder he's paranoid about keeping people he can control here." Duff pulled up beside the *Edwina*. He killed the engine and climbed off so he could face her.

"So you believe me?"

Lightning illuminated the clouds, followed by a thunderclap. Melanie huddled inside the poncho and snapped her gaze up into the sky. "You do know a clearing where there's water is probably the last place we should be in this storm?"

"The fiberglass hull won't conduct electricity. Right, Nature Girl?"

"Really? Another nickname?" But she nodded. "Only in salt water. Dad said it's the salt clinging to the hull that's actually conducting the electricity. This is a freshwater lake. We should be safe."

"I knew you'd have the answer. Come on. I'm tired of getting wet." He held out a hand he hoped she would take. He could tell by the tilt of her eyes that she was deciding whether or not to accept the amends he was trying to make. The next clap of thunder hastened her decision. She linked her hand with his and he led her to the upturned boat to take shelter beneath the gunwale. They weren't completely out of the elements, but the fiberglass frame protected them from the wind and the worst of the deluge. With his back against what was once the bottom of the boat, he sat on the edge of the storage well and pulled her onto his lap. "I need you to listen to me."

"I get it. You're some kind of spy. That's why you wanted to be my friend. You need me to get close to Henry or you think I know something about those guns. I don't." She leaned back against his chest, draping the poncho over both of them. "I understand the need to lie when you're working undercover. But friendship wasn't enough? Why did you pretend you were interested in something more?"

"Because I *am* interested in something more." Duff's arms snuck around her waist before he realized she was snuggling closer out of practicality, not because she'd forgiven him. With that sweet baby scent of her wet hair filling up his nose, he had to close his eyes against the desire to nuzzle the shell of her ear. "I'm not a spy. I'm a Kansas City cop. You can't tell anyone who I really am or why I'm here." The irony of what he was about to ask wasn't lost on him. "Can I trust you to keep my secret?"

"Can I trust you not to lie to me again?"

Lightning forked from the sky, striking a distant tree. When Melanie jerked against him, he tightened his hold on her. "You got a thing about storms?"

"My father died on a night like this."

He felt her relax and adjust herself to a more comfortable position. He stifled a groan as her bottom nestled against his groin. She was seeking honesty and comfort, not the passion she sparked inside him.

"The violence reminds me of that night. Thunder woke me and I went to Dad's room. He wasn't there. I never saw him again."

He could imagine the little girl's terror had doubled when the one person she counted on wasn't there for her. Melanie kindled something far more potent than passion inside him. He hurt for that little girl who'd never gotten the answers she needed to understand why her daddy wasn't coming home. "I'm sorry."

Hugging her tight against his chest, Duff gave in to the need to taste her. He nosed aside her hair and pressed a kiss to the cool skin at the nape of her neck. Her answering shiver moved through him, stirring needs and desires.

When she tilted her head to give him access to more of that creamy expanse, Duff obliged by lapping up each droplet of water clinging to her skin, and lingering on the warm pulse beating underneath. "This is where I feel closest to Dad," she murmured, giving him the smooth line of her jaw to explore. "Life here was a part of who he was. We spent so many wonderful days on or beside the water." She tipped her head forward, pulling her hair over her shoulder and wringing it out beside her. "That probably sounds childish."

He was far too aware of his forearm caught beneath the weight of her breasts, and how badly he wanted to fill his hands with them. But this embrace was about rebuilding trust, and maybe even earning her forgiveness. So he pressed a chaste kiss to the base of her neck, cooling his jets. "Makes sense to me."

He watched the charcoal-gray water and whitecaps slapping against the bobbing dock as the lake churned with the storm's fury. Even as his body warmed with the woman sitting on his lap, his thoughts strayed back to the city and to memories that were equally turbulent. His grandfather's unconscious, bleeding body. A shooter disappearing into the snow.

He let his thoughts drift farther back in time to that fateful night when he'd seen his father crying for the first time. He wasn't entirely aware of his arms tightening around Melanie, but he was aware of when she shifted in his lap so that she could see his face. "What is it?"

He thought he smiled, but it was probably more of a scowl as those long-buried emotions surged inside him. "The night at the hospital when Dad told me Mom had been shot—she never even made it into surgery. I remember being so angry. I didn't believe him. I jumped in my car and drove like the crazy teenager I was to the convenience store to see the crime scene and police cars and blood for myself."

A hand on his shoulder allowed him to continue.

"I thought I could find Mom there—that Dad and the other cops just hadn't looked hard enough. That

the woman in the ER was someone else." He pulled
his gaze from the lake and his thoughts from the past
to look into whiskey-brown eyes that glistened with
tears. Duff caught one tear with his thumb before it
joined the raindrops beading on her cheek. "I drove
by that store nearly every day for years, always with
some irrational thought that one day she'd be there."
He caught the next tear, too, and found the pain of his
past easing with Melanie's empathy. "Even though
the place has been torn down and built into a drug-
store, I drive by that corner every now and then. So,
yeah, I get why this place means so much to you."

And then Melanie Fiske, the woman who was one
surprise after another, framed her hands around his
jaw and sealed her lips against his. Her kiss was as
tender as it was bold. He didn't need to teach her a
damn thing about what turned him on, about what
touched his heart. The woman might be inexperi-
enced, but she was a natural talent and Duff needed
everything she was willing to give him.

He tunneled his fingers into her hair, tilted her
head back and opened his mouth over hers, sliding
his tongue between her lips to claim her heat. She
slipped her arms around his neck and lifted herself
into the kiss. Her breasts pillowed against his chest,
their lush shape imprinting his skin through the wet
clothes between them. His hands fisted in her hair as
his body caught fire with the need to consume her
caring and passion. Each foray of her lips, each skim
of her hands against his neck and hair, each husky

moan deep in her throat was like tinder to the desire burning through him.

He spread his thighs, giving the response she triggered in him room to swell behind his zipper. She dragged her hand between them, he thought to push him away because he was moving way too fast for her. But she brushed her fingers over the taut button of his nipple in a curious caress, and he groaned as his skin jumped. Perhaps startled by his eager response, she turned her mouth from his. "I'm sorry. I didn't mean to pinch—"

"It's all good. That reaction means I like what you're doing." He pulled her fingers back to his chest. "I *really* like what you're doing."

"If you're lying to me—"

He reclaimed her mouth, telling her as succinctly as he could that this was no act. She made the pain of his past go away. She made him believe he could trust a woman again, that he could allow himself to need her. She must have gotten the message. Because her hand slipped lower, and when she tugged his shirt from his belt to slide her hand against bare skin, he thought he might explode.

Duff moved his lips to the point of her chin, to her eyelids and the tip of her nose before coming back to claim that sensuous mouth. He battled with the bulky poncho to get his hands inside her clothes to explore her the way she was learning his body. Her cool skin heated beneath his touch, and she stretched to give him access to each delectable curve. He flicked his thumb over the straining tip of her breast through the satiny material covering it and felt her jump in response, just as he had.

"It feels good, doesn't it," he murmured against her mouth. She nodded, burying her face against the side of his neck. "How about this?"

He palmed her breast, lifting its bountiful weight in his hand. He skimmed the backs of his fingers beneath the stretchy material of her bra, capturing the pearled flesh between his fingertips and palm. Melanie gasped his name, tilting her passion-glazed eyes up to his.

"Say it again," he whispered, lowering his head.

"Tom." She pushed herself into his hand.

"Again."

"Tom—"

He reclaimed her mouth, savoring the rush of her response. *Incendiary* was the only word that flashed in his mind when he thought of the two of them together. Melanie didn't need to be experienced—she just needed to be his.

He'd just found his way to the clasp of her bra when he heard the snap of a twig.

Swearing against her lips, he pulled his hands from her clothes, shifted her against his side in a one-armed hug and reached for his gun.

Chapter Ten

A swath of dripping brunette hair swung into view before Deanna Fiske came face-to-face with the barrel of Duff's Glock. "Whoa!"

She backpedaled a step, colliding with Roy Cassmeyer when he came around the edge of the boat. "Now what?" Roy saw the gun, grabbed Deanna and reached for his own weapon.

"I wouldn't do that, son," Duff warned. The wary alertness pounding through Duff's veins didn't want to dissipate.

"No, sir." Roy put up both hands, leaving the gun strapped at his waist. "We didn't mean to startle you." He glanced over at Melanie as she straightened her clothes. "Or interrupt."

"You two alone?" Duff asked.

"Yes, sir." Roy must have realized his hands were still up in surrender because he pulled them down to his side. "Sorry, Mel. I never figured you… We were looking for a place to get out of this rain."

Duff grabbed Melanie before she bolted like a skittish colt and anchored her to his thigh as he lowered his weapon. "You know better than to sneak up on a man, Roy." He slipped the gun back into its holster and prayed that Melanie wouldn't say or do anything—either accidentally or intentionally—that would give away his real identity and purpose for being here. He inclined his head, inviting the two twentysomethings to duck under the rusted over-hang of the old boat's windshield. "What are you two doing out in this mess?"

Deanna giggled as she squeezed in beside Roy. "Same thing you are. Mom will never believe me, Mel, when I tell her you're here, making out with Duff. And there I was, offering you pointers. You're always about books and work and 'I miss my daddy.' I'd never have guessed that you knew how to give a man a little sugar."

Duff thought he'd choke on the treacly sweet barbs Deanna was dishing out.

Before he could shut her up, Melanie pointed to the gun Roy was wearing. "Do you always carry a gun on a date? Is my cousin really that much trou-ble?"

Direct hit. Duff couldn't help but grin. Give him a woman with a brain and a backbone any day. He was already falling a little bit in love with Melanie's unique blend of fire and innocence, with her com-mitment and compassion. But he was proving to be a total sucker for that wicked sense of humor.

Deanna arched a dark eyebrow, maybe miffed that Melanie hadn't folded at her taunt. "Duff has a gun. Doesn't it make you feel safe to be with an armed man?"

"I'm on security detail," Duff reminded the skinny little flirt who needed to watch her mouth, especially those not-so-sly digs at Melanie.

"Uh-huh." Now that was a brilliant comeback.

Melanie straightened the hair he'd tangled in his hands, then splayed her fingers at the center of his chest. Was she taking over the charade of two lovers who weren't very happy to be discovered? "Is there a reason I shouldn't feel safe out here?"

"No, ma'am," Roy answered. "The security around the farm is really tight. Silas makes sure of that."

And yet the young man was still packing a gun. Did Henry think his daughter needed protection from something out here in the woods? From someone? Why wouldn't Duff have been informed of any particular threat to look out for, unless Henry and Silas didn't want him to know about whatever Roy was up to? "Where have you been?"

"Boat dock."

"Nowhere."

"You two want to get your answers straight?"

Roy draped his arm around Deanna's shoulders, glaring down at her. But, apparently, she couldn't take a hint. "I surprised Roy at the boat dock. He was out on the water. Barely made it in before the storm hit. I thought we could warm each other up, but he insisted we leave—"

"Shut up, Deanna."

"Don't tell me to—"

"There's a storage shed at the boat dock," Melanie pointed out. "You could have used that for shelter."

"That's what I said," Deanna pointed out, poking Roy in the stomach.

Roy straightened, about to spew some well-rehearsed line. "I wanted to get Deanna home. You know how spotty cell reception is out here. I didn't want Henry and Abby to worry."

"There's a landline in the storage shed," Melanie reminded him.

Roy's cheeks colored like bricks. "I forgot."

Duff needed to check that dock and the boat Roy had been on. He liked the kid, and would hate to discover he was part of the smuggling operation. But, whether Roy was innocent or not, retracing his activities tonight, before Silas or Henry knew Duff was onto them, meant squaring things with Melanie and getting the two lovebirds out of the way. "The storm's letting up." He pointed to the hills to the west. "Home and dry clothes are that way. You'll still get wet, but it should be safe to travel."

Roy assessed the sky, as well, before nodding. "We'll leave you two alone."

He reached for Deanna's hand. But she pulled against him. "I don't want to go home. I snuck out to see you, and you've been in a snit ever since I got here."

"I told you not to come see me tonight." Deanna stumbled when Roy tugged her to his side. "How am I going to explain to your daddy that you missed curfew?"

"They don't have to know what we were doing."

"We weren't doing anything."

"Whose fault is that?"

Duff stood, snagging Melanie's hand to balance her as he dumped her from his lap. "I've got a flashlight on the ATV. Take it—if you two don't mind walking. We'll use the headlight to find our way back."

"You won't tell Mom and Dad you saw me, will you, Mel?" Deanna asked. "Of course not. You snuck out to see a guy, too. I won't tell, either."

"Maybe you should get going," Melanie urged her cousin.

"Ooh, they want to be alone. Take your time. I know we will." Deanna giggled until Roy shushed her.

"Thanks, Duff." Roy grabbed the flashlight and pulled Deanna into the tree line with him. "You're embarrassing me. Now come on."

"Embarrassing you? You know, Roy, I know a dozen men who would love to—"

"Seriously. Can't you be quiet for two seconds?"

Once the bickering young couple was out of earshot, Duff turned to Melanie. "I'm sorry about what Deanna said. You don't need pointers from anybody."

Melanie pulled her hand from his, hunching her shoulders against the weather as she headed toward the ATV. "She wasn't lying about my lack of experience. You were hurting. I wanted to comfort you. I didn't really know what I was doing. It's okay, Duff."

He caught her hand and pulled her back to face him. "Uh-uh. Duff's a nickname I've had since I was a kid. I want you to call me Tom. Just like you have been. It's my real name." He moved his hands to clasp her shoulders and waited for her to tilt those pretty brown eyes up to his. "Thomas Watson Jr. I'm a KCPD cop, just like my father and grandfather before me. Only one other person ever called me Tom. But I'm getting used to hearing it from you. I like it."

The thunder had ebbed to a soft rumble. "We'd better get back to the farm, too. The last thing we need is someone sending out a search party for us," Melanie said.

Duff tightened his grip on her arms. "This isn't a part-time thing that you turn on and off when we have an audience. You never know when someone will be watching. If we're going to do this, then we have to work like a team. You have to commit to this mission twenty-four/seven."

"I get it. Didn't I cover for you all right just now?"

"You did great, Doc." Duff watched the rain hitting her freckles as she waited for him to choose his next words. "But I feel like you're pulling away from me. That something your twit of a cousin said is making you doubt me. What happened here wasn't any kind of training session or test run. I know other men have taken advantage of your connection to Henry—put the moves on you without meaning it. But other than the fact I lied about my last name and why I'm here, there's not a thing that's happened between us that hasn't been real. Think about the chemistry between us instead of the charade—"

"You don't have to sell me. I understand what

teamwork is." She pushed at the middle of his chest, and this time he let her move away. "I can do this. I *will* do this."

"It could be dangerous. If I'm found out, your uncle—"

"I know. He'll sic Silas on us. Or something worse."

He had a pretty good idea of what *worse* could mean. His stomach churned at the idea of anyone hurting Melanie that way. If it wasn't for that curiosity of hers, he'd never have put her in this position of becoming an undercover operative with him.

She needed to understand the consequences the same way he did. "Whether anything comes of you and me, I need your word that you'll protect my identity and the real reason I'm here, or I'm going to walk away right now and you'll never see me again." He caught a cord of her auburn hair between his thumb and forefinger and toyed with the curly wet silk before cupping the side of her neck. "I don't know how much more honest I can be. My life is in your hands."

After several long moments when he wasn't sure what she was going to say or do, she turned her cheek into his palm, sending a rush of reassurance up his arm to nestle close to his heart before she pulled away. "I'll keep your secret. I won't tell anyone about your meeting place by the old fire tower. I'll help you get the information you're looking for. If you're ever unaccounted for and someone asks where you've been, I'll cover for you." And then she broke the contact between them and backed away. "But you have to do something for me."

"You want me to help investigate your father's death." He nodded, already planning to do at least that much for her. He followed her to the ATV. "If anything on my case leads to information about your father, I'll share it."

"Can you get your doctor brother back here to take a look at SueAnn?"

"He's not that kind of doctor. Niall is with the crime lab." When she started to protest, he put his hand up to stop her. "Okay. Maybe Niall knows enough to help her."

"And you'll take me to Kansas City with you when you leave. Once I find out about Dad, I'll have no reason to stay here."

"You're already compromising my mission just by knowing—"

"Escape to KC or no deal."

The woman struck a hard bargain. Still, he needed her to maintain his cover and help him find the weapons. "All right. It might mean a hasty exit if things go south—as in drop everything and run when I tell you to—but I promise to get you out of this place when my mission's over. Deal?"

"Deal." She extended her hand to shake his.

But Duff wasn't ready to go back to being just friends after what they'd shared a few minutes earlier. Hell, he was still half-hard with need, and that soft, smushy place around his heart didn't seem to be toughening up any when it came to the stubborn redhead. So he took hold of her hand and helped her climb on to the ATV seat behind him. "Want to check out the boat dock with me? Roy might have been running an errand for Henry—setting up for a drop-off, making a delivery."

"With Deanna there? Henry wouldn't risk her safety."

"It sounds as though their meeting wasn't planned. Maybe Roy wasn't expecting to find Deanna there."

"Or she wasn't expecting to find him and covered with her usual sexy shtick. Is she smart enough to be a part of this?" Maybe Melanie's armor wasn't completely back in place, either, because, instead of clinging to the sides of his belt the way she had on the ride here, she wrapped her arms around his waist.

Duff allowed himself a few seconds to relish the gesture of trust before he started the engine and headed toward the gravel road. "You think that bimbo routine is an act?"

"I wouldn't have thought so, but so many things have changed around here lately, I can't be certain."

"Wouldn't be the first time someone used an innocent to help mask his crimes, either. Look at meth labs in suburban family homes or children used as suicide bombers."

"There really *is* something awful happening here."

"Something awful enough that innocent people in my city are being hurt because of it. People in my family are being hurt."

"Your family?"

"KCPD believes a gun smuggled through here was used to shoot my grandfather." The rain had filled the ruts with water, forcing Duff to slow his speed so they wouldn't slide into a ditch. "Grandpa was enjoying my sister's wedding the day he got shot. His spirit's tough, but his body is fragile. He may never be the same."

"He survived?"

Pain, anger and a burning need for retribution filled his soul, just like the rain soaking the earth. "Barely."

"I'm sorry." Melanie's arms squeezed around his waist, and that dark desperation inside him seemed to dissolve along with the storm. "I'll show you a way to the boat dock without taking the main road."

"Thank you."

"For showing you a shortcut?"

"For keeping my secret."

He turned in the direction she'd indicated, ducking his head to dodge the low-hanging branches that masked the path beside the lake. Other than telling him where to turn, Melanie was silent for another quarter mile before she spoke again. "Who called you Tom?"

"My mom."

Her grip around him loosened and she sat back. "Then maybe I shouldn't."

Duff grasped her hands to keep them linked together. "I never asked anyone else to."

"Tom, I—"

"Yeah. Just like that." Hearing his name in that husky tone was pretty heady stuff for a man who'd sworn off relationships. He stopped the ATV and let the engine idle while he turned halfway around on the seat. "Maybe you've been right all along about the nickname thing. When you say *Tom* it sounds like you're not as mad at me as you thought you were."

"I'm not mad. I just… I wanted you to be real."

"Trust me, Doc, what I'm feeling for you is real. I thought I had this place all figured out—that you were all part of some country-bumpkin mafia. I never figured on someone like you being here. You're a distraction I wasn't planning on."

"I'm no kind of distraction." She laughed, but it was a self-deprecating sound that made him a little ticked off at Deanna and the people who had made her feel that way.

"Don't sell yourself short, Doc, er, Melanie."

"It's okay. I'm getting used to hearing you call me that, too."

"You will be a doctor one day. If anyone can come from where you've been and earn all those degrees, you can. I'd bet money on it." He loved seeing her blush at the compliment. He'd never known a woman so responsive to a word or touch. He prayed to God he was putting his faith in the right woman this time.

He bent his head to capture her wet lips in a kiss. When she reached up to cup his cheek and return the kiss, Duff's eyes drifted shut, and he drank in her sweet scent and eager mouth, knowing he was falling harder and faster than a smart undercover cop should. There was confusion in her big, brown eyes that matched the emotions roiling inside him when he pulled away. But there was a sound of satisfaction in her sigh that echoed through him, calming his doubts…for the moment. He released her and repositioned himself on the seat before shifting the engine into gear. "You got my back on this?"

"I've got your back." She rested her cheek between his shoulder blades and held on tight as they sped around the lake.

MELANIE WAS RIGHT about the shortcut. In a matter of minutes, they popped out of the trees onto a man-made beach and approached the modern aluminum boat dock along the edge of the water. After parking the ATV, Duff pulled out his cell phone and switched it into flashlight mode. He followed Melanie up the rocky embankment and slipped beneath the metal railing to reach the stairs that led up to the parking lot and storage shed or down to the boathouse and covered dock where two power boats bobbed up and down in the slips where they'd been tied.

Duff took the lead and headed down the stairs. "Do you know which boat Roy would have been on?"

"Probably the *August Moon*. We usually rent the *Ozark Dreamer* out to tourists."

Unlike the quiet cove where the *Edwina* was beached, this place was all about modern amenities. There were four slips in total, one rigged for docking power skis. There were canoes stacked on racks inside, too, along with equipment cabinets and life vests. Melanie opened a toolbox sitting on one of the shelves and pulled out a flashlight.

"I think this is where Deanna was waiting for Roy." She knelt beside a wadded blanket and an over-turned cooler and pulled out a can of soda pop, in-dicating the contents before setting it upright and closing it again. "Looks like they left in a hurry. I understand wanting to get away from the water with the lightning—but why not grab their stuff and go up to the storage shed to wait out the storm?"

"It seemed to me like Roy was a lot more anxious to leave than she was."

"What are we looking for?" Melanie asked, pok-ing around inside the canoes and equipment.

Duff walked out along the gangway and peered inside the *August Moon*. "Guns, ammo and cash would be the obvious thing, but that's probably too easy. Anything that looks out of place. Storage com-partments that look like they've been recently dis-turbed." Duff spotted a trio of scratch marks on the aft fishing deck of the *August Moon*, and climbed on board for a closer look. "Tracks along the shore, in case Roy hauled something off the boat."

They explored the area for several minutes. Duff snapped pictures of the scratch marks and a smear of some gelatinous goo on the gunwale that hadn't been washed away by the rain or the waves. Fish guts? He found a deeper gash on the fishing deck it-self, as if someone had tried to butcher a fish or cut something loose.

He heard a soft gasp before Melanie called out to him. "Tom? I found something."

Duff vaulted over the side of the boat and hur-

ried to the last slip on the dock. He swore like the
man's man he was when he saw the decomposing
dead body caught halfway beneath the dock, bobbing among the cattails.

He reached for Melanie, palming the back of her
head and turning her into his arms, away from the
nibbled-on bones and bloated, peeling skin wrapped
in a long black coat. "Ah, hell, Doc. I never wanted
you to see something like this."

The leather belt binding the arms to the body,
and the shreds of rope tied to the wrists and ankles,
indicated that this was no accidental drowning. Although Duff and the task force had suspected that
the people involved in the gun smuggling were capable of murder, he hadn't expected a dead body to
be the type of evidence he'd find.

Melanie's fingers clung tightly to the front of
Duff's soggy T-shirt, but short of wrestling her to
the ground, she was determined to look at the distorted body. "He's been dead awhile, hasn't he?"

"I'm no forensics expert like Niall, but I'm guessing the body has been submerged for a couple of
months, give or take." He wondered at the marks he'd
seen on the back of Henry's boat. Had Roy discovered the body, too, and tried to hide it from Deanna?
Or were those cut marks and the fraying ropes indicators that Roy had been trying to dispose of the
body? "The storm must have stirred it up from the
bottom of the lake."

Melanie's grip on him eased and she turned her
light back to the boat he'd been inspecting. "Or it

got caught on the *Moon*'s propeller." As the dock bobbed with the waves, the boat and lift rose above the water, giving him a glimpse of frayed rope caught in the propeller blades.

"Hold that light steady if you can." If she was willing to play detective with him, and it kept her focus off the dead body, Duff was going to put her to work. While she held the light, he got down on his stomach and took several pictures before plucking a few rope strands free and stuffing them into one of the plastic bags left in his pocket. Maybe Roy had accidentally snagged the body and had tried to cut it free. "The rope looks like a match."

"You should take pictures of the body, too. Before he floats away—" she cringed "—or falls apart."

"Wait for me in the boathouse while I get it up onshore." With her father's drowning, this was probably the last crime scene she needed to be around.

But either that endless curiosity or red-haired stubbornness had kicked in. "Don't be such a tough guy. I can help."

"It's not a tough-guy thing. I'm trying to look out for you."

"There'll be cadavers in med school."

Not like this one, he'd wager.

Maybe speed was the kindest thing he could do for her at this point—get this awful task out of the way so that she could move on to something less gruesome. He pointed to the poncho she was still wearing. "We'll use that."

While she stripped off the poncho and spread it

on the ground near the dock, Duff waded into the water and carried the body to the shore. He set it on the poncho and pulled one corner over the poor guy's ravaged face so Melanie wouldn't have to look at it. While he checked pockets for a billfold and identification he suspected he wouldn't find, she pointed to a hole in the chest of the long, black duster that was holding the main part of the body together. "That's a bullet hole, isn't it? Right through his heart."

"Looks like it."

She pointed to the belt that had been tied, not buckled, around his torso and arms. "If this is his belt…" Before he could stop her, she touched the two ends of the swollen leather square knot. "This hasn't been chewed on. It's been cut. Where's his belt buckle?"

A really bad feeling washed over Duff, rocking him back on his heels. His brother Keir had identified their grandfather's masked shooter by a one-of-a-kind fancy belt buckle in pictures he'd taken during the ambush at the church. And the man Duff had chased across the roof had worn a long black duster. If the gun had come from the Fiske farm… If this man was the killer hired to destroy his family…

"Tom?" He snapped his gaze over to Melanie, startled from his thoughts by that sweet husky voice. "We have to report this," she said.

He needed to talk to his family. Pronto. This could be the connection they'd been looking for. Duff raised his phone up to the moonlight peeking through the lingering clouds, hoping to see bars of connectivity here. "One of us will have to stay with the body while the other gets to a phone."

"There's one in the shed."

"I'd prefer to use a secure line that won't show up on your uncle's phone bill."

"You can't call Agent Benton. That'd give you—us—away if he and a crime scene team showed up here."

"I don't want to give anyone a chance to move it. We're still out of cell range. I need to get back to the fire tower or find a private spot in one of the main buildings to notify my team." He pushed to his feet, climbing a few steps up the embankment. "I need you to call Sheriff Cobb. You can use the shed phone for that."

"What if he's part of the smuggling operation? What if Cobb already knows there's a dead body in the lake and hadn't planned to do anything about it?"

"I'll get word to the task force. They can keep an eye on Cobb and whatever he does or doesn't do."

But Melanie wasn't listening. "It's hard to be sure, but this coat looks familiar."

"You know this guy?" Duff pocketed his phone and jumped down to the shoreline behind her. There wasn't enough of a face to identify, and the fingerprints would be long gone. Maybe Melanie had spotted something he hadn't.

"SueAnn's brother had a coat like this. It would have been cold enough to wear one when he went missing. You don't suppose…" Now that he was done taking pictures, Melanie pulled the edges of the poncho over the dead man's body. "This will kill SueAnn. With her blood pressure, I don't know if she could handle the stress of finding out Richard's dead."

"If it *is* him. Let's not jump to conclusions. We have to identify him first." Duff watched her rise to her feet and stumble back to the edge of the dock. Her normally telegraphic skin was as pale as the moonlight. Forgetting the potential link to his grandfather's case, his task-force mission and the urgency of getting word to his family, Duff knelt beside her to peer into her eyes. "Doc? What's wrong?"

She dragged her gaze from the corpse back to Duff. "Is this what happened to my father, too?"

Chapter Eleven

Everyone Melanie knew from the farm and Falls City seemed to be gathered near the fishing dock as the sun came up. Everyone except for Tom, who'd left to place a call to Agent Benton, and SueAnn, who was dealing with a lack of sleep and explicit instructions from Melanie not to be disturbed.

Although she was praying that the dead body down on the shore wasn't Richard Lloyd, Melanie had a bad feeling that Mother Nature had uncovered one secret that the farm had been hiding. Yet, with one revealed, a dozen more seemed to hover in the air around her.

Roy and Deanna sat in his pickup at the top of the embankment, looking as miserable as Melanie felt. Her own jeans and shirt were still damp, and sticky now that the sun was warming the air. Apparently, Roy had admitted to snagging the body on the boat. That explained why he'd been so anxious to get Deanna away from the fishing dock. But why hadn't he reported it? And why had he been out on the lake so late in the first place? And if this did prove to be murder, would Henry or whoever was responsible make Roy the fall guy for the crime?

Henry was on the dock with Silas and Sterling Cobb. Silas seemed more concerned about the dock bobbing beneath him than with the hushed conversation. His fist was wrapped in a haphazard bandage that was stained with dried blood. The rifle she'd seen him wearing at the house was missing from his shoulder, as were the gun and knife that were usually strapped to his waist. Had she ever seen the bald man unarmed before? Did his weapons have anything to do with the bullet hole in the dead man's chest, or the ropes and belt binding the corpse's limbs? And would the sheriff appreciate her pointing out that he'd been wearing leather gloves in July, possibly hiding that injury to his hand the night before last? She had a strong feeling that Silas wouldn't.

And what about the bespectacled paramedic who'd shown up with the coroner's van and was helping a deputy and another paramedic zip up the body and load it onto a gurney? Although it had been dark and rainy last night at the old fire tower, she was certain that the dark-haired man with a ball cap pulled down low over his forehead was Tom's brother. She didn't think she should strike up a conversation with him, but as she glanced around the crowd of onlookers standing behind the yellow crime-scene tape, she wondered if Tom knew his brother was here—if there'd be a surprised recognition between them that would be hard to hide from Henry, Silas or the sheriff.

And where was Tom, anyway? Clearly, he'd had time enough to contact his task-force handler and his brother. She'd told the sheriff that she and Tom had been at the dock looking for shelter and privacy when she'd discovered the body and called it in, and had let Sterling Cobb fill in the blanks about why they'd been together and what they'd needed privacy for.

How far would that kiss-and-grope session at her father's boat have gone if Roy and Deanna hadn't interrupted them? Had she ever let down her guard like that with a man before? Had she ever felt that crazy sort of hunger, that connection to another person's soul?

She'd wanted to stay mad at him for lying to her. But he'd touched her heart, instead, sharing the story about coping with his mother's death, truly understanding her pain. She'd meant her kiss to console him, to promise she'd never betray to anyone those painful emotions they shared. But that chemistry he mentioned had flared between them, instead, and getting closer—learning his body, absorbing his strength, feeling his caring surrounding her—suddenly felt like the only way she could ever feel normal or safe again. She'd been ready to straddle Tom's lap and give him access to whatever he wanted from her, so long as he never let her go.

Until Roy and Deanna's arrival had reminded her of the reality at hand. Storms and secrets. Lies and danger. Falling in love with Tom Watson had no place in her world.

Melanie shivered. *Falling in love?* Is that what was happening to her?

Tom had comforted her, argued with her, made her laugh and gotten so far inside her thoughts that she was having a hard time reconstructing the defensive barriers that had sustained her these past several months. She hadn't needed anyone for a long time. But she needed him.

But was his tender concern for her really about *her* and not a fear that she'd reveal he was working undercover?

Despite her confused feelings, she wanted Tom to be here. Except for the undercover medical examiner, whom she didn't think she should talk to, she felt alone right now. And ever since Tom had barged into her life, become her friend and forced her into an alliance that could get them both killed, the one thing she hadn't felt was alone.

"Melanie, dear?" She startled at the arm around her shoulder. Aunt Abby's hug lasted about as long as it took Melanie to identify the older woman. "My goodness, your clothes are still wet." Abby rested the back of her knuckles against Melanie's cheek in a display of maternal concern. "You'd better come back to the main house with me so you can change out of these things before you catch cold."

She probably did look like a drowned rat with her soggy clothes and hair that kinked and expanded as it dried in the humid air. But a shower and dry clothes and her aunt's momentary compassion weren't going

to make the unsettling fact that there'd been a murder in their little utopia go away. "I have to stay. I
found the body. The sheriff said he may have more
questions for me."

"Sterling will wait if your uncle asks him to."

No doubt. "I'd rather get it over with."

"I understand you were out here last night with
Duff. Awfully late, from what I hear." Melanie
couldn't help but slide her gaze up to the parking
lot where Roy and Deanna were parked. One or both
of them had tattled. Probably to divert attention from
their own late-night return. "Where's your new boyfriend this morning? I'm sure Sterling will want to
interview him, too."

"Boy—" Melanie clamped her mouth shut to sti-
fle her protest. A couple? Lovers? Was that the story
Tom expected her to tell to anyone who asked? The
dock rocking beneath her feet wasn't the only thing
throwing her a little off-kilter this morning. "I'm a
grown-up. I don't have to account for where I spend
my time. Or who I spend it with."

"Being a grown-up and understanding what a man
wants from a woman are two different things."

Melanie bristled at what sounded like the beginning of a birds-and-the-bees lecture. "I understand
Tom well enough. He likes being out in nature. And
I like being with him." That wasn't a lie. She *could*
do this. "He enjoys the quiet of the night."

"Last night was anything but quiet."

In more ways than one. Melanie swayed as the

wake from a Conservation Department powerboat searching the area rolled to the shore beneath them. "We couldn't exactly plan the weather, now, could we?"

"That explains why you were at the lake last night." Abby squeezed Melanie's forearm, practically tutting her tongue against her teeth in an expression of pity and concern. "But where has Duff gotten off to now? Leaving you to deal with this unfortunate mess all on your own. If he really cared about you, he'd be here to support you."

So the sheriff's questions could wait, but not her aunt's? Melanie took a couple of steps toward the edge of the dock to watch Tom's brother and the deputy carry the body bag up the stairs to the parking lot. "Look at all these people. He hates crowds."

But Abby wouldn't let her subtle accusations against Tom drop. "You don't find it strange that he ducked out on you like this? Do you know where he is right now? How do you know he didn't kill that man?"

She whirled around on her aunt. "Because *that man* has been dead a lot longer than the time Tom, er, Duff, has been here."

"You don't have to defend me, sweetheart. I'm right here." The deep, growly voice behind her was like music to her ears. Tom wrapped a big flannel shirt around her and briefly clasped his hands over her shoulders. "I couldn't find a jacket so I grabbed this out of my bag. Hope it doesn't make you too hot."

"Thanks." Fighting the urge to fall back against

his chest and let him deal with her aunt's sniping, Melanie summoned the remnants of her own strength. Although flannel wouldn't have been her first choice for something dry to cover up with, she was pleased that he'd thought of her discomfort. Or maybe coming back with one of his big shirts was just the excuse he was using to cover his absence. She discovered the motive didn't matter. After rolling up the long sleeves, she snuggled into the oversize shirt. The brushed cotton smelled like Tom, and she found its warmth and scent as reassuring as the brush of his hands on her shoulders had been. Masquerade or not, she breathed a tiny sigh of relief, knowing she was no longer alone with a gathering full of potential enemies.

When she turned to truly thank him, she realized he was wearing a different T-shirt. His jeans were dry, too. "You changed."

"The clothes I had on when I fished John Doe out of the lake were pretty gross. I talked to one of the guys with the coroner's van and gave the stuff to him." His brother, Niall, she assumed. So part of the delay in returning to her had been about him being a cop doing his job. "I thought they'd want to bag it since there might be some evidence from the corpse on it, too."

"Bag it? Gross? Corpse?" Abby hugged her arms around her waist. "You two may have hearts of stone, but I can't deal with this. Especially if he turns out to be Richard. Whatever will we tell SueAnn?" She turned to the three men still conversing on the dock beside the boat. "Henry, dear, could you drive me back to the house?"

"I'll do it, sir," Silas volunteered. He pushed past the sheriff, touching his injured hand to Abby's elbow, no doubt anxious to get as far from the water as he could.

"I'll take care of my wife, Silas," Henry declared, motioning the big man to stay put. He handed the sheriff a paper evidence bag that a civilian probably shouldn't have been holding in the first place and moved between Silas and Abby. "You and Sterling make all this go away. Understand? Dead bodies are bad for business."

"Yes, sir."

Henry's gaze bounced off Melanie and centered on the top of the hill. He leaned back and snapped another order at Silas. "Tell Roy to report to my office as soon as the sheriff is done with him. And make sure my daughter gets safely home."

"We'll take Deanna home with us," Abby announced.

Resigned to being their messenger boy for the time being, Silas latched on to the nearest post as the dock shifted with Henry and Abby's departure. But Melanie was less amused by his anxiety as she focused in on the plastic window in the bag Sheriff Cobb was holding. She could see the stiff, mutilated belt that had been tied around the victim's body. She wondered if he'd given any thought to the odd piece of evidence. "Sheriff, did you look at that belt?" She pointed to the distorted leather than had been sawed through. "Don't you find it strange that the body was tied up with it?"

Sheriff Cobb shrugged. "Tool of opportunity, I imagine."

"But why remove the buckle?"

"Maybe this is a robbery gone bad. I remember that shiny silver thing Richard used to wear."

"So you think it's Richard, too." She found her courage enhanced by Tom's presence behind her. "We don't know that yet, do we?"

Silas muttered something under his breath. "Maybe the buckle just got in the killer's way. It's probably down at the bottom of Lake Hanover."

"What did the buckle look like?" Tom asked.

"Why do you want to know? Are you investigating this case?"

Tom shrugged, refusing to be baited. "I want to know so I can keep a lookout for it on my patrols. In case it washes up somewhere. Maybe there'll be fingerprints on it that could tell you who killed him, Sheriff."

"I appreciate having another set of eyes out here." Sterling Cobb seemed unaware of the tension between the two men. "Richard wore a unique belt buckle. So maybe you're right, Mr. Maynard. It could help identify that this is him. If we can match it to the belt." The sheriff rested his elbow on the butt of his gun as he sorted through his memories. "That buckle was silver. Had some gold or brass on it. Made him look like he was some kind of rodeo cowboy."

Melanie turned to the sound of footsteps hurrying across the dock behind her. Daryl Renick wasn't smiling as he joined them. He pointed to the carved silver buckle with a brass spur emblazoned on it at his own waist. "It looked just like this. Minus the notches for each of his kills."

"Kills?" Tom and Melanie echoed together.

"He had a list of animals he wanted to hunt. Every time he bagged one on his list, he carved an *X* on his buckle."

Sheriff Cobb chuckled. "That boy always was a cocky son of a gun, wasn't he?"

"Could I take a picture of that, Daryl?" Tom pulled out his phone, and Melanie's concern flared for an instant. Would Silas or Sheriff Cobb see the dozens of pictures Tom had been taking around the lake and farm?

"I don't care, but make it fast." Daryl's dark eyes barely acknowledged the click of Tom's phone as he turned to the sheriff. "I want a look at that body. Word is it's Richard. I want to see him for myself."

"You're not going to be able to identify him by looking at him. He was in the water a long time," the sheriff warned.

"I knew him better than anybody here. I know what clothes he was wearing when he disappeared. If there's anything in his pockets, I could identify it. Please." Daryl's scruffy face was lined with worry, and Melanie reached over to squeeze his hand. He said, "My wife can't take much more of not knowing what happened to her brother. Even if the news is bad, if I can tell her that Richard's been found…"

"Is SueAnn all right?" Melanie asked.

"She woke up having those fake contractions again. They stopped. But this…" Daryl's fingers pumped around hers. "Maybe you'd better come check on her when you get done here."

"I will. As soon as I can."

Sheriff Cobb seemed to understand the urgency of the situation. "We'd best get up the hill and talk to the coroner before he leaves, then. They want to take the body to Kansas City 'cause we don't have the proper facilities here. I don't mind them takin' a dead body off my hands. But if you want to see it… Silas." He nodded to the farm's security chief before tipping his hat to Melanie. "Miss Fiske. I'll call if I need anything else from you."

Daryl hurried up the steps to the parking lot, and Sheriff Cobb followed more slowly after him. Melanie's concern shifted from SueAnn to Tom. The lines beside his eyes had narrowed into a frown. He stared at the image on his phone as if he'd seen a ghost.

Before she could ask what was wrong, though, Silas's mocking voice reminded her Baldy was still there. "Something eatin' at you, Sergeant?"

"Tom?" He had gone quiet. Too quiet. Had he just pieced together something about his case? No matter what, she wasn't about to let Silas goad him into revealing something he shouldn't. She could buy Tom a few seconds of distraction while he cleared his thoughts and remembered he wasn't supposed to look as though he was playing detective. Since she was already in medic mode, she turned to Silas and nodded toward his injured hand. "Do you want me to take a look at that cut? Looks like the bandage hasn't been changed for a while."

"I'm fine." Silas pulled his hand away from the post, flexing his fingers. "You didn't answer my question, Sergeant Loser."

She, on the other hand, had been playing detective for months now, and felt right at home pointing out suspicious details. "How did you cut yourself? Is that why you had gloves on the other day? To hide that wound?"

Silas blinked, and when he opened his dark eyes again, they were focused squarely on her. "A working man wears gloves to protect his hands." No farmer she'd met wore black leather driving gloves to toss a hay bale or fix a barn roof. Not that she'd ever seen Silas do either of those jobs. Before she could challenge him on evading the question, he snagged her by the wrist with that same bandaged hand. "I'll pick you up tonight for the dance."

"I told you I'm not—"

"No, you won't." Tom was back with her. His phone was back in his pocket as he pried Silas's hand off her. While Silas shook the feeling back into his hand, Tom slid his arm around her shoulders. "She's going with me."

Silas grinned. "You've got patrol duty tonight."

"Not until ten o'clock. She's with me until then. Afterward, too, if she wants." When Silas opened his mouth to argue, Tom poked his finger into the middle of the bald man's chest. "And if you put your hand on her like that again, I'll break it."

Chapter Twelve

Melanie curled her toes into an eyelet-trimmed pillow, stretching herself awake on the love seat where she'd dozed off. She blinked the bent page of her book into focus in the dim light seeping through the curtains and frowned.

After a rain-soaked night without sleep, she'd been anxious to get into a hot shower and fall into bed for a long nap. But finding a dead body, imagining her father suffering a similar fate, and discovering just how much she wanted Detective Thomas Watson Jr. to be more than a friend and coinvestigator, had all crept into her head, haunting her dreams and forcing her out of bed to find a story she knew had a happy ending. Not that it helped much. Asleep or awake, those images and worries and wishes were still with her.

"Melanie?" A sharp knock on her door startled her and she leaped to her feet, realizing an earlier knock had wakened her in the first place.

Smoothing the crumpled page of *Jane Eyre* back

into place, she closed the book and hurried to the door. "What's the emergency—"

The door swung open before she could reach it, and she jumped back at the sight of Tom filling her doorway. "Damn it, woman, why don't you answer...? Are you okay?"

Melanie nodded, retreating a step as he closed the door behind him.

The anger that had narrowed his eyes dissipated at her unblinking stare. This wasn't soldier Tom or loner Tom or sexy Tom... Well, okay, to her way of thinking he was always *sexy* Tom. But this was a new version of the man she was getting to know. He'd shaved, revealing all kinds of interesting angles along his carved cheeks and rugged jawline. And he'd put on a white button-down shirt that hugged his shoulders and arms as nicely as a T-shirt. Plus, he'd removed the shoulder holster he always wore. This was date-night Tom.

Date-night Tom?

"Aren't you ready?"

Melanie snapped her gaping mouth shut. "You were serious about going to the dance?"

"As a heart attack." He plucked the book from her hands and set it on the table beside the lamp. "This shindig started five minutes ago. Now throw on something pretty and let's go."

She stumbled along in front of him as he scooted her toward her bedroom. "I thought you said that to put Silas off about hounding me to go with him.

I thought we were going to do some investigating while everyone was out at the barn."

"You're right on both counts." He grabbed her hand and pulled her into the bedroom when she apparently wasn't moving fast enough. The momentary shock of having a grown, sexy, date-night man in her bedroom for the first time heated her skin with excitement. But she didn't get much time to blush. For one thing, he was still wearing his gun, although he'd tucked it into a holster at the back of his waist, reminding her of their undercover charade. Secondly, Tom released her and walked straight to her closet and opened it. He thumbed through the meager selection of blouses and jeans, looking for a fancy dress that didn't exist. Maybe she shouldn't have begged out of that shopping expedition with her aunt and Deanna. "We can't sneak out of a social event unless we put in an appearance first. And if we don't show at all, your aunt or uncle will send someone to look for us. That's the last thing we want." He pulled out the sleeveless turquoise cotton dress that she'd worn for her graduation from Metropolitan College four years earlier. "Here. Do this one."

He was no more a fashionista than she was. But Melanie understood the pressure of time. She snatched the hanger from his hand, pushed him out the door and changed. She slipped on a pair of flip-flops and hurried into the bathroom next door, frowning at the smashed bed-head look she'd accomplished when she'd fallen asleep on the couch with wet hair. After running a brush through it without much success, she braided the curls into a long plait.

She was dabbing on some lip gloss when she realized Tall, Dark and Date-Night was watching her work. Tom leaned his shoulder against the door frame while his gaze took a leisurely stroll from the top of her head down to her toes and back. "You've got legs, Doc."

She capped the lip gloss and dropped it back into a drawer, facing him with a wry smile. "Two of them, as a matter of fact."

Even as he laughed, he reached out to capture the end of her braid between his fingers and tugged her toward him. She stopped herself from tripping by bracing her hands against his chest. She marveled at his masculine shape, then moved her fingers across the crisp cotton covering his sturdy muscles and warm skin. He trembled when she flicked her fingertips over his taut nipple. Or maybe she trembled at the knowledge she could induce that helpless reaction from him. His voice dropped to that growly rumble she loved. "You are built like nobody's business."

"That's good?"

"That is *so* good." When his mouth touched hers, her lips were already parting, hungry for his kiss. She might not have a long track record with this kind of thing, but he was an excellent teacher, and she'd always been an eager student. He nipped at her bottom lip, then eased the excited nerve endings with the raspy stroke of his tongue. She mimicked the same nibble and stroke on his firm mouth and he groaned. "I'm the one who said we had to make an appearance, right?"

She never got a chance to answer.

When his tongue slid into her mouth, hers darted forward to meet his. His hands left her hair to pull her arms around his neck, and then he was sliding his hands down her back, moving closer. He palmed her butt and pulled her onto her toes, bringing her body into the hard heat of his as his mouth opened possessively over hers.

Just as she thought she was getting the hang of all the touches and tastes that triggered that husky growl in his throat, he tore his mouth away and moved his hands to frame her on either side of the doorway. His chest heaved with a mighty breath, rubbing against her breasts, making her whimper as a jolt of electricity shot through the tips and cascaded through her like stars falling straight into the needy heart of her. Tom captured her mouth in one more chaste kiss before pulling her fingers from the collar of his shirt and grasping her hand. "We need to go now, or we never will."

MELANIE WAS BREATHLESS by the time they finished the two-step and applauded the band, which was stopping for a short break. After sharing several dances, she was beginning to think of tonight as a real date. Feeling Tom's body move against hers, knowing how secure the grip of his hand was around her own, hearing him laugh and talk about everything—from how he'd learned line dancing from his grandpa in an attempt to impress a girl in college to speculating about who had given Roy a black eye—made Melanie feel as if they'd known each other much longer than a couple of weeks.

Although she was still anxious to leave the Fiske Farm behind her and do more with her life once the ghost of her father was laid to rest, she was rethinking the idea of independent spinsterhood. She simply hadn't met the right man until Tom had barged into her life. Tom 'Duff Maynard' Watson made her happy. He made her hope. And even if he was just a good guy who lusted after her a little and cared about her like the good friend he'd become, she knew she'd never regret falling in love with him.

Melanie stumbled over her own bare toes as the truth hit her.

Before she could glance up to see if she was broadcasting her feelings with a telltale blush, Tom tugged on her hand, pulling her past the punch bowl where Silas was doctoring his lemonade with a shot from his flask. Tom scooped up a cup of the untainted drink, taking a sip before handing it to her. Silas scowled in their direction, but she realized the condemning look wasn't aimed at them, but at Abby and Deanna Fiske, who were chatting with the band's bass player and lead singer. Henry joined them, wrapping an arm around each woman's waist and saying something that made them all laugh.

My, what a show her aunt and uncle were putting on for the tenants and staff who worked here. Maybe they were eager to take everyone's minds off the news of the dead body. Maybe they were showing off their wealth and success. Either way, they seemed oblivious to Silas's grumpy mood and to Roy lurking in the shadows near the door like a dog who'd been banished from the house for the night.

Melanie didn't have time to ask Tom if he'd observed what she had. Instead, he picked up her flip-flops from beneath their table and pushed them into her hands. He dipped his mouth beside her ear. "Giggle."

"What?" She held on to his arm for balance as she slipped the sandals onto her feet.

"Laugh like I said something clever and you can't resist me."

"Tom…"

"That'll do." He grinned a split second before moving his mouth over hers in a quick, hard kiss. "I don't know why that's such a turn-on. Time to make our escape."

"You want me to pretend like I can't wait to be alone with you?" Catching on to the subterfuge, she did her best imitation of Deanna's flirtatious giggle.

Tom made a face at the silly, high-pitched sound. "Never do that again."

Melanie laughed out loud, grabbed her phone off the table and followed him out of the barn.

Tom traded a nod with Roy before taking a circuitous route across the compound to avoid anyone's notice. Once assured that the main house was empty, she and Tom entered off the back deck and made a beeline for the stairs. He hurried her up to the second floor, keeping watch while she lowered the attic steps. The stuffiness of the room nearly stole the air from her lungs. She pointed to the window in the back wall. "You want me to open that?"

He stopped her hand when she reached for the overhead light. He picked up the two flashlights on the shelf near the top of the steps and handed one to her. "The light and an open window might draw someone's attention. We can sweat for five minutes. I figure that's about how long we've got before we need to be seen somewhere else. Let's make this fast."

Nodding her understanding, Melanie set her phone on the shelf and switched on her flashlight to lead him across the room to the metal shelves. She shined her light on the box of her aunt's rodeo queen memorabilia and frowned. "Someone else has been up here since my last visit." Everything had been stacked in neat rows on the shelves again, blocking the wall behind them. "What if they cleared out the room because I was snooping around? I hope I didn't mess up your investigation."

He squeezed her shoulder. "We find what we find. But only if we look."

Melanie nodded. "The door's behind there."

Tom lifted the shelves, contents and all, creating a space big enough for him to slide behind. "Light," he ordered. Hurrying to do his bidding, she joined him and shined her light on the padlock as he knelt in front of it. He had a special tool in his back pocket that made quick work of the lock. He stuffed the padlock and tool into his pocket and opened the door. "Son of a bitch."

Melanie couldn't squeeze between the shelves and door fast enough to see inside the room that was no bigger than a walk-in closet. "Oh, my God."

She swung her light around, counting the heavy black bags stacked two deep against one side of the tiny room. On the wall opposite the door stood a set of shelves that held boxes of ammunition, cell phones still in their packages and what looked like several bundles of cash, stacked and wrapped like cubes in sheets of clear plastic. The last wall had several broken-down shipping boxes labeled with an innocuous Lake Hanover Freight stamp leaning against it.

Tom pulled a rifle from one of the bags. He pointed to the small black ring anchored to the middle of the barrel. A gas block. Just like the one she'd found on her father's boat. Melanie felt sick to her stomach. This was happening, right here, in the house where she'd grown up. "Children live on this farm. Thousands of innocent people come through here all summer long. How can there be so many guns? How can this be safe?"

"It's not."

Leaving Tom to snap pictures as he emptied first one bag, then another, Melanie moved over to the shelves to study the items there. "There must be thousands of dollars here."

"Tens of thousands. Maybe more." He opened the next bag and laid the guns on the floor. "I'll call

Benton. I can text him these images from here. Go back to the opening and keep an eye out for visitors. I need to document the serial numbers on these weapons to confirm that they're stolen or unregistered before they get sanded off. This may take longer than five minutes."

Her eyes widened when he pulled a roll of adhesive tape out of the pocket of his dark-wash jeans. "You come prepared for anything, don't you?"

"Borrowed it from Henry's office." He tore off a length of tape and pressed it to the trigger assembly of one of the handguns. "I'm no CSI, but if I can pick up any kind of prints—"

"Then you can prove who's smuggling them."

"You said you saw Silas wearing black leather gloves the other day?"

"Yeah. Then he had a bandage on his hand this morning."

Tom snapped a photograph before pulling something from inside the bag of weapons. "Did it look like this?"

He held up a leather glove, shining his light on it. She knelt beside him, studying it. "That's blood."

"The leather's been sliced through, too."

"Somebody was using a knife on the *August Moon*. Cutting ropes to tie up that body? Removing the belt buckle that could identify Richard? You don't think Silas had something to do with that dead body, do you?"

"I do." He dropped the glove into a plastic bag and stuffed it into his pocket. She wondered when he'd raided her infirmary for supplies again. But then, she supposed there were some mysteries about this man she would never fully understand. "Whether he was cleaning up someone else's mess—or he was responsible for the murder itself, I can't say."

"Someone else's mess? Like Roy's? Do you think *he* was trying to dispose of the body? Maybe Deanna surprised him before he could get it on or off the boat. He didn't seem too happy to see her last night."

"That could explain the black eye. Either he screwed up his job, he wasn't supposed to find that body, or whoever he reports to—Silas or Henry— punished him for letting Deanna anywhere near it."

Bracing her hand against Tom's sturdy thigh, Melanie pushed to her feet. The cubes of money were as fascinating as they were disturbing. On closer inspection, she discovered they, too, had labels printed on them. They each had dates and initials—KC, SL, DC—money from Kansas City? St. Louis? Denver, Colorado? Or being paid out to…whom? Silas Lou Danvers? Deanna Christine Fiske? Could her self-absorbed cousin really be involved in something like this? Her curious thoughts took a sideways turn when she read a label that had no initials. "Isn't a Gin Rickey a drink?"

"What did you say?"

Surprised to feel Tom's heat beside her, she pointed to the dusty label on the cube of money. *Gin Rickey.* She heard an audible gasp as his shoulder sagged against hers. "Tom, what's wrong? You know what this means, don't you?"

"It's the code name for a hired killer."

"A hired…? Someone here…?"

"My brother Keir—he's a detective, too—was looking into another case and discovered the code name for a hit man. One of the contact numbers led to this part of the state." He swiped his palm over his jaw, scratching at the smooth skin as though searching for that perennial beard stubble that was usually there. A fist squeezed around Melanie's heart. That was pain, not anger, she saw in his expression. "The man who shot my grandfather. The man we could only identify by—"

"A belt buckle like Daryl's." She reached up to cup the tight line of Tom's jaw. "The body in the lake… You think he shot your grandfather. You think someone hired Richard Lloyd to shoot your grandfather."

"Rickey? Richard?"

Unfortunately, it made sense to her, too. Richard's disappearance. His hunting expertise. The odd jobs Henry would send him on. All this cash. "This money was used to pay Richard to kill…?"

Tom pressed a kiss into the palm of her hand before going back to work. "We need the crime lab to ID that body. Not that it does me much good. Lloyd had no reason to come after my family. I never met any of you before I came here."

"It's not like you can ask who hired him. And why kill him? Who shot Richard? The person who hired him?"

"The best way to cover your tracks is to eliminate them." Tom shrugged. "Either that, or he screwed up the job. Maybe Grandpa was supposed to die. Or one of us was. Or we all were."

Melanie's stomach tightened with fear. "Could someone here know you're a cop? That you're from a family of cops?"

Tom went utterly still for a few moments before resuming his work. "I haven't seen indications that anyone suspects me. Except you. You were the only one curious enough to find out. More likely your uncle or Silas just sold Richard's services."

"For all this money." She shook her head. Tom had once joked that he was looking for some country-bumpkin mafia. Apparently, she was living right in the middle of it. Silas and Roy were relatively new hires. But Richard would have been a child like her fourteen years ago when her father died. How long had these criminal activities been going on at the Fiske Family Farm? Had Leroy uncovered the same secrets she and Tom were discovering now? Had Henry silenced his own brother to protect those secrets?

Melanie was about to share her suspicions with Tom when she heard the smack of the screen door slamming below their feet. Dashing to the top of the steps, she trained her ear to the stomps and mutters she could hear from the first floor. "Someone just came in."

Tom was right beside her, exchanging his phone for his gun.

She heard another door, followed by the clink of

glass against glass. "Whoever it is went into Henry's office."

There was a slur of angry words—and then a second clink. Someone was pouring a drink. Or two. "Think you're too good for me." That wasn't her uncle's voice. A board creaked beneath Melanie's flip-flop and she froze. "Somebody there?"

Not her uncle. Something much worse.

She turned to Tom, dodging his hands as he tried to pull her away from the opening. "How much longer do you need?"

"No." He was answering a question she hadn't asked.

"How long to finish cataloguing all that evidence and get it to your friends?"

Tom was shaking his head, reaching for her as she backed away. "It's not worth—"

"We might not get a second chance."

"Doc—"

"Do your job." She descended the attic steps and pulled on the rope, closing the door into the ceiling. "Do it fast."

She tiptoed down the stairs.

Chapter Thirteen

Melanie was nearly to the bottom step in the main hallway when Silas lurched out of Henry's office. He was twisting the lid onto his flask as if he'd just refilled it at her uncle's liquor cabinet. When his rheumy gaze landed on her, she offered him a polite smile and hurried past him to the front door.

He grabbed her arm, stopping an easy escape. "What are you doing here, girl?" He stuffed the flask into his hip pocket and eyed her like a tipsy vulture. "Sergeant Loser dump you?"

She couldn't help but glance up the stairs, relieved to see no sign of Tom. He'd face much worse than the lecture she'd received if he was caught in the attic. Quickly averting her gaze, she tugged against Silas's grip. "No, I was just—"

"Headin' back for the comfort of your old room? Need a shoulder to cry on?" Silas's fingers tightened painfully around her upper arm and he pulled her to him. She thrust her hand against the center of his chest to wedge some space between them. But even half-toasted, his strength easily overpowered hers.

She squeezed her eyes and mouth shut as he pushed her face into his shoulder. "I knew there was something wrong about that guy. He ain't one of us."

She didn't want to be one of them, either. And she certainly didn't want or need any comfort from this bully. Melanie mentally ran through all of the release moves Tom had shown her at their morning defense lessons to end this embrace. Going limp and bending her knees, she sank out of Silas's arms before he could tighten his grip. But, again, her freedom was short-lived. He clutched her by both arms this time.

Her attempt to stomp on his instep merely tripped him and they crashed into the wall together. Maybe she could talk her way out of this. "Would you still like to dance with me tonight? I hear the music starting up again at the barn. We should go."

"I'm tired of dancin' to your tune, Deanna, darlin'." His breath reeked as he nuzzled the side of her neck. The hand at her waist slid over her hip to pull up the hem of her dress. "Leadin' me on like a trained dog."

Melanie slapped his hand away and twisted out of his grasp. "You're drunk. I'm not Deanna."

Clarity didn't help. He slammed his hand against the wall, blocking her path. "Maybe taming you would make things interesting, after all. Where is that boyfriend of yours, anyway? Couldn't he get the job done?"

"Silas…" The fear that colored her voice at his crude suggestion morphed into a whole different type of fear when she heard a scraping sound two floors above them. Silas tilted his face up the stairs. He'd heard it, too. She needed to cover for Tom. She'd promised to have his back. He needed to be safe. Swallowing her disgust, Melanie touched Silas's cheek and turned his bald head her direction again. *Run, Tom.* "Um… Maybe I do need a shoulder to cry on. Could you just hold me?"

"Sure thing." He forgot the noise with a lascivious grin. Instead of a hug, Silas grabbed her and pushed her against the wall. Melanie knew she was in trouble when she couldn't get the behemoth to budge. "You got that sensible underwear on tonight, Mel?" Bile churned in her stomach as Silas's hands ran over her. She couldn't find any comfort in knowing he was no longer confusing her with another woman. "Doesn't matter. Naked's the way I like my women. I'll make you forget all about him."

Melanie panicked at the assault, blanking on every trick Tom had taught her. She was helpless to do more than scream in her mouth as Silas ground his lips over hers, filling her mouth with the taste of stale whiskey. He thrust other parts of his body against places she'd never wanted him to touch.

For a brief moment, she knew that if she mentioned Tom was in the house, she could get away. Silas would leave her to confront the intruder. She could save herself if she sacrificed Tom. But she'd seen all those guns upstairs. She'd seen Roy's black eye. She'd seen a decomposing body. If Silas found out Tom was a cop and he'd found evidence to link him to those crimes, she'd be finding Tom's body floating in the lake with a bullet hole in his chest.

That couldn't happen. She couldn't let the man she loved be hurt by these people.

But she couldn't stand one more second of Silas pawing at her, either. She'd find another way to get away *and* help Tom escape. She wrenched her mouth away from Silas's. "Let go of me!" She scratched her fingers over his scalp, startling him into drawing back. She shoved the butt of her hand up against his nose and heard a pop.

He grabbed his face and tumbled backward. "You bitch!" Anger and pain must have cleared his foggy brain enough to see her running down the hall. After just a few steps, his hand clamped over her wrist, jerking her back into the hard slap of his hand across her cheek. Melanie's knees buckled as white dots swam across her vision, blurring her senses to a banging sound and a shouting voice. Silas shoved her up against the wall. "You uppity, teasing—"

A massive forearm closed around Silas's neck and dragged him away from her. Suddenly free, Melanie collapsed against the wall. Silas kicked his feet and clawed at the bulging muscles that were choking him. Blood dripped from his nose onto the rolled-up white sleeve. She blinked her eyes clear to see Tom's furious expression as he strangled his prey.

"Tom! Tom, stop!"

Silas's bloody face turned red, then purple. His struggles became little more than flailing hands. Then his arms dropped to his sides, his eyes closed

and he went limp like a rag doll. Silas's bulky frame
bobbed up and down as Tom heaved several deep
breaths. Melanie looked up into Tom's narrowed
green eyes and found them burning through her.
"You okay?"

She pushed herself up straighter and nodded. "Is
he dead?"

"No. But he'll be out for a few minutes." He
glanced up and down the shadowed hallway. Had
any of them screamed or cursed loudly enough for
someone to hear them? "You up to helping me?"

Again, she could do little more than nod.

"Grab his feet."

Melanie pushed away from the wall and lifted Silas's heavy boots after Tom shifted his grip beneath
the big man's arms to haul him into Henry's office.
Adrenaline was still pumping so hard through her
system that it was hard to concentrate. "What are
we doing?"

"Creating a plausible reason for him to be passed
out here." Tom dumped the unconscious body onto
her uncle's leather couch. She positioned his feet
while Tom pushed him onto his side to retrieve the
flask from Silas's back pocket.

"When Silas comes to he'll tell Henry about us.
You should get out of here. You should get in your
truck and just leave."

"I'm not going anywhere. And he won't talk." Tom
opened the flask and poured the amber contents all
over Silas's shirt and the couch. "Getting drunk on
the boss's whiskey and passing out in his office isn't

going to earn him any brownie points. If he wakes up before he's discovered, he'll leave to cover his tracks. If he's discovered here, he's got too big of an ego to admit he lost a fight." He tossed the flask onto Silas's sleeping body. Tom's fingers curled into a tight fist at his side. "I'm sorry I didn't get here sooner. I could hear what was happening and… I'm sorry." He reached over to lift the braid of her hair off her shoulder and Melanie flinched. "You're not okay."

The adrenaline must be wearing off now because she was suddenly so chilled she was shaking.

IT WAS THE second time Duff had seen Melanie charge across the compound into her cottage, desperate to escape the toxic hell of her family and so-called friends. Although she'd avoided his touch, at least she didn't slam the door on him this time, shutting him out of her pain and anger.

To think that that bastard had hurt her…to realize she'd put herself in that position to protect him… The rage at seeing Silas strike her was still coursing through him. But Melanie didn't need rage right now. She needed… Well, hell, he wasn't sure what she needed, but he wasn't about to walk away and let her deal with Fiske family crap on her own. He didn't plan to leave her alone again until they were miles away from this place. And, even then, he didn't think he ever wanted to be far from her.

Still, when she marched straight to the sink and turned on the water to soap up her hands and arms, he quietly closed the door and waited for her to vent.

She didn't. She dried off her hands, then turned on the water again to wash her face. "How did you get past Silas?"

"Didn't have to. I climbed out the attic window and dropped onto the roof of the back porch. Shimmied down that oak tree shading the porch from there." When she started rinsing out her mouth, as well, Duff had to go to her. He picked up the towel she'd tossed onto the counter and handed it to her.

She dabbed at her face. "And then you circled around the house to come in the front door. That's good thinking. No one will suspect we were in the attic."

When she put the towel down, Duff saw the red handprint on the side of her face and cursed. Her brown eyes widened with surprise, but instead of apologizing for startling her, he reached for her hand and led her into the infirmary. When she protested his caveman need to protect his woman, he grabbed her by the waist and lifted her onto the examination table, warning her to stay put while he searched for an ice pack. "Damn it, Doc. I feel like I'm always on the wrong side of saving you."

"What are you talking about?"

He fumbled with the ice he pulled from the mini-fridge but, eventually, forced several pieces into a towel before folding it into a rudimentary packet. "When Silas puts his hands on you or Deanna insults you or I know your brain is making comparisons to dead bodies that have to be breaking your heart—I want to protect you from all that."

"It could have been worse. You taught me how to fight him."

"It wasn't enough."

"I'll be okay."

"I know. Because you're brave and resourceful and stubborn to a fault. You're so used to saving yourself…" He gently pressed the ice pack to her bruised cheek. "But can you blame a guy for wanting to keep someone he cares about safe?"

"You couldn't have stepped in to stop Silas any sooner—not without giving away why you're here. We both heard you moving the shelf in the attic, although I think he was too drunk to know what it meant." She reached up to cover his hand with hers, holding the ice pack in place, cooling the protective rage inside him, too. "I need you to succeed. I need you to put these people away. Forget about Dad. You have to stop the guns and the violence."

Uh-uh. He slipped his fingers into the hair behind her ears, tilting her turbulent brown eyes up to his. "I'm not forgetting anybody. Once we get the players into custody, they'll be willing to talk. I'm not giving up on your father. We'll get these guys—as soon as the lab gets back to us, the task force should be able to obtain warrants. I'll put them away in prison and then I'll take you away from this place. I promise."

She nudged him back a step and this time he let her hop down off the table. "Did you find what you needed to solve your case?"

"Yes." He followed her through the cottage to her bedroom, where she opened the top drawer of her dresser and pulled out her father's watch. "We'll have to play this game out another day or two. We can't let anyone know what we're up to until my team is ready to move in. Otherwise, Henry and Silas will move the guns again, and we need to catch them with the evidence. Can you handle that?"

She nodded, but he didn't quite believe her. "What's next? Another rendezvous at the old fire tower?" She ran her palms over the hips of her dress, searching for a spot to put the watch. "I should put on a pair of jeans."

Instead of changing, she scurried around him into the bathroom. Duff put the watch in his own pocket to carry it for her. She dumped the ice into the sink, inspecting the mark on her face before dabbing at her face and lips with the towel. She turned her back to him and pointed to her zipper. "Can you undo me? I want to shower."

Instead of undressing her, he wrapped his arms around the top of her chest and pulled her to him, hugging her from behind. "You're okay, Doc."

She struggled only momentarily before sagging against him. "I know. I mean, in my head, I know I'm okay." She reached up to hold on to his arms. "But I got really scared tonight."

"I know, babe. I'm so sorry." He pressed his lips to the crown of her hair. "You want to get out of here?"

"Kansas City?"

Duff tightened his hug. "Not yet. But I've got an idea. My truck is parked out in the parking lot. Trust me?"

A few minutes later they were bouncing over the gravel road that led to the old dock. The moon was bright enough that any time they cleared the canopy of leaves and branches, he got a glimpse of Melanie's face. To his relief, the farther they got from the compound, the more color he detected on her freckled skin. She rolled down the window to breathe in the fresh night air. "This was an excellent idea. I'm feeling better."

If she was strong enough to listen, he had something he needed to say. "You could have told Silas I was upstairs. You could have told him I'm a cop and what I'm doing here. He'd have come after me instead of you."

"I thought about it," she admitted. "But I wouldn't have had your back very well, then, would I?"

Duff knew right then and there he was in love with this woman. He reached over to capture her hand in his. "Yeah, Doc. You had my back."

They drove in bumpy silence several more minutes until they reached the old dock and the wreck of the *Edwina*. After parking the truck, he untied his work boots and toed them off, tossing them into the back of the truck, along with his socks and belt. He locked his gun, wallet and phone in the gear box and untucked his shirt. Catching on to his intent, Melanie tossed her flip-flops into the bed of the truck and grabbed the old blanket he kept rolled up behind the seat. Then they walked hand in hand out to the edge of the dock, spread the blanket out to protect them from splinters and sat, dangling their feet in the water that was still warm from the afternoon sun.

The moonlight bathed Melanie's skin with an angelic glow and reflected off the lake, but the trees surrounding the cove still provided a feeling of privacy. The water lapped quietly in the grasses on either side of them, and splashed up to their ankles and calves with every gentle sway of the dock. A symphony of cicadas and frogs serenaded them.

"It's like an IV for you out here, isn't it?" He loved watching her flex her legs and splash her toes in the water. "Feeling better?"

"This has always been a special place." She leaned closer and rested her cheek against his shoulder. "I like it even better that you're sharing it with me."

"Just trying to have your back." Her wet toes came out of the water to slide beneath the rolled-up hem of his jeans to tickle his leg. His entire body warmed at the brush of her skin against his. Yep, he was totally gone on this woman. "I wish I'd been able to get to you sooner tonight. When I said I needed your help, I never meant for you to have to…" He muttered a choice word, then kissed her hair, apologizing for bringing anything harsh into this peaceful place. "I want to bust that jackass's face again for touching you."

"*I* want to bust his face. You know, you never did show me how to do a good old-fashioned uppercut." She studied her fist in front of her for several seconds before she drew her hand back to her heart. "It was different than when you touch me."

"I hope like hell it was." Duff pulled his right leg out of the water, stretching it out on the blanket behind her so he could face her. He cupped her face between his hands and leaned in to kiss her.

He'd meant it to be a gentle reassurance. But when she fisted her hands in the front of his shirt and pulled herself up into the kiss, parting her lips and sneaking her tongue out to meet his, he forgot about gentle. Her husky groan ignited his own hunger, and he slipped his hands down, trying to pull her into his lap, closer to the male part of him that always responded to her passion. But the angle was awkward and the dock was rocking and he needed her to understand the difference between his touch and Silas's.

With a groan of his own, he tore his mouth from her lips and rested his forehead against hers. He ran his hands up and down her arms. "I can't keep my hands off you because you excite me. You challenge me and frustrate me and make me laugh and make me crazy. You make me want to talk about things I never talk about." Her warm, whiskey-colored eyes looked up into his, and she looked so gorgeous that he couldn't help kissing her again, taking his leisurely fill of her mouth, then touching his forehead to hers again. He needed her to understand. He needed her to believe his words. "There's a difference between control and desire. Between respect and using. You need to know how special you are. How beautiful. And if any man doesn't make you feel that, he doesn't deserve you."

She flattened her palms against the sandpapery new stubble that was itching his jawline again. Her lips curled into a bemused smile as she rubbed her hands over his cheeks before sliding them around his neck to caress his short hair. Duff's blood heated with anticipation, even as he held himself still beneath each provocative touch. He idly wondered if she knew what she was doing to him, if she could hear his heart thump faster in his chest or feel the quickening rhythm of his breath stirring her hair. She drew her fingers tenderly over his shoulder to rest beside the healing wound there. "I love the way you kiss me. And I like…" His eyes narrowed, waiting expectantly as her wicked hands danced across his chest. "I like exploring how you feel under my hands. You're all different textures and hard planes and vulnerable places and…" Her blush intensified. "I love how your hands make me feel, too, and… I want you to show me what it's like when a man cares. If you're interested."

Oh, he was interested. Very. More than he should be. But he needed her to be sure of what she was asking of him. He touched a fingertip to the blush climbing up her neck. "Am I your first?"

Melanie nodded. "First kiss. First date. First time." That blush intensified, just like the emotions burning inside him. "I'm twenty-five years old. Does that make me a freak?"

Duff caught her chin in his hand and tilted her face to his when embarrassment made her look away.

"It makes you special. I can't tell you how honored—and how scared—it makes me to be your first."

"Scared? Of having sex with me?"

"Of making love to you," he clarified. "I want it to be a good memory for you. I'm scared I'm not up to the task." He tugged her braid between them and pulled the rubber band from the end before slowly unwinding her hair. "Anything you don't like…anything that frightens you…you tell me. I'll make it right. Or I'll stop. Whatever you need."

"I wouldn't trust anyone else with the job."

Her husky vow was as much of a turn-on as it was a reassurance. "Yeah?"

"Yeah." He fanned her hair around her shoulders and sifted his fingers into the thick, sexy waves. "I need you to kiss me now."

He needed that, too. Once their lips met, conscious thought flew out of his brain and instinct took over. She wound her arms around his neck and crawled up his body, pushing her breasts against his chest. They pebbled and poked him and his hands were there in an instant, squeezing their weight and rolling the tips between his thumb and hand until she was panting "more" against his mouth.

The woman had rock-solid instincts, too. She tugged at the buttons of his shirt and pushed the wrinkled cotton off his shoulders. He was groaning for more when she palmed his pectoral muscles and started playing with his responsive flesh. He unzipped her dress and wriggled it off over her head, hating that he lost contact with her lips but consoling himself by pressing a kiss to her abdomen and the underside of her breast and the fine line of her collarbone as every inch of her was slowly revealed to his hungry gaze.

The dress joined his shirt somewhere on the dock and then they were skin to skin. Melanie crawled into his lap, straddling him. Her fingers brushed against his stomach muscles and trailed lower, tugging at the snap of his jeans. Her thighs squeezed around his hips and he rocked himself helplessly against her feminine heat. This was going too fast. She might think she was prepared for this, but he couldn't simply strip her naked and bury himself inside her without making sure she was ready for him.

"Trust me?" he whispered against her mouth, chasing her lips as they grazed along the column of his neck, eliciting tiny little shocks of electricity that threatened his resolve.

With her nod, he wound his arms tightly around her and leaned over the edge of the dock, pulling her into the water with him. There was no startled gasp, no cold shock, only the tightening of her arms and legs around him. The warm water sluiced in between them, and for a few seconds Duff simply held her, treading water and enjoying the rocking motion of the waves around them, tempering the desire pounding through him. He moved his hands along her arms and back and around the thighs that wrapped his waist, gently bathing her, washing away any memory of Silas's hands on her.

Once the frantic energy radiating off her dissipated, they swam around for a few minutes, splashing each other, sneaking kisses in unexpected places, laughing and playing tag and kissing again. Melanie was like a water nymph, with her long hair floating in the water around her, hiding the best bits from his appreciative gaze until she moved and he caught a glimpse of a breast or bottom as she darted from his touch.

A breathless Melanie grinned as she reached behind her to unclasp her bra. "I've never been skinny-dipping with someone else before. Aren't we supposed to be naked?"

So much for cooling his jets. The weight of his wet jeans pulled his feet down to the solid bottom, but he was standing on shaky ground as she bared her beautiful breasts to him and the moonlight. Suddenly, Duff was hungry and impatient. The water couldn't temper his need any longer. When she made a token effort to swim away, he caught her by the ankle and pulled her hard against him, lifting her breast to his mouth and capturing the tip in a needy suckle. She moaned, splaying her fingers at the back of his head, holding his mouth against her.

"Tom…"

"That's the magic word." He carried her to the ladder at the edge of the dock and climbed up after her. He snatched up their discarded clothes and pushed them into her arms to cover herself. Then he grabbed the blanket and her hand and hurried back to his truck.

The time it took to spread the blanket in the bed

of his truck, form a makeshift pillow from their dry clothes and peel off their wet ones was far too long to be apart from this woman who'd gotten so far into his head and under his skin that the only way he could feel right again was to let her into his heart. Once he'd rolled on a condom and she was reaching for him, Duff settled between her knees and pushed himself inside her. He hesitated when he reached her tight barrier. But this sexy, brave woman was having none of that. She dug her fingers into his spine, angled her hips and urged him to fill her. She winced and buried her face against the juncture of his neck and shoulder as she stretched to accommodate him. Stars dotted the inside of his eyelids as her body gripped him. He was dangerously close to losing himself inside her.

But Duff held his breath, held her. "You okay?"

"I think I'm more okay than I've been in a long time. I've never felt this close to anyone before. This feels…right. But…" Was it possible for a woman's entire body to blush?

"But what?" His arms shook with restraint as he propped himself above her. "You know you can tell me anything."

"Aren't there supposed to be bells and whistles?"

Duff's laugh echoed through the clear night air. "Yeah. Very definitely." Her eyes drifted shut as he reclaimed her lips and moved inside her. "Bells and…" Together they found a rhythm that rocked them as sweetly as the waves on the lake. And when the whispers of his name turned into silent, needy gasps, he pressed himself against that sensitive bundle of nerves and felt her detonate around him. "And whistles."

He swallowed up her husky cry with a kiss. And with the waves of her pleasure convulsing around him, the combustion hit him, too.

Afterward, he collapsed atop the blanket and pulled her into his arms beside him.

Melanie snuggled close, tangling her legs with his and pushing her hair out of her eyes. The dampness from the lake and their loving cooled his skin as their heavy, stuttered breaths synced and slowed. She settled her cheek against the pillow of his shoulder and whispered, "Wow. I liked the bells and whistles. A lot."

"Me, too, Doc."

He pulled the edges of the blanket over them and hugged her close. The peal of imaginary bells rang in his thoughts as Melanie drifted off to sleep, while Duff watched real stars dot the night sky above them.

Chapter Fourteen

Melanie couldn't decide which she liked better—the powerful, beautiful and cherished feelings from Tom's lovemaking, or the quiet, intimate talks they shared in between. She loved that he was a snuggler as much as he was a fighter, and that he could touch her heart with his growly words as well as he could kiss her and make her body feel things that, well, she'd only read about in books.

She was slightly winded from her second lesson in seduction, and feeling the grooves of the plastic truck bed liner digging into her hip, but she wasn't going anywhere. Not as long as the night was clear and Tom wanted to hold her. Toasty warm against his side, she traced figure eights through the crisp curls of brown hair that dusted his deep chest and smiled. "So that's the deep, dark secret about your nickname? A bike wreck when you were ten?"

His assent rumbled through his chest. "I kept trying to tell everybody in the hospital how 'tough' I was after breaking my nose and getting my front teeth knocked out after going stuntman off that rock wall behind our old house. But with my injuries, I couldn't say the *T* sound, so it came out 'Duff.' Since I was prone to taking a risk or two, the name stuck."

"A risk or two?"

"I've been to the ER more times than my brothers, sister and father combined."

Melanie's fingers stilled above his heart. "I don't think I like those statistics."

He captured her hand against his chest. "It's okay. I'm tough." He chuckled. "Or, I should say, I'm *Duff*."

She smiled at the story from his childhood. "I don't think you're as 'duff' as you claim. I saw how you felt when you talked about your mother. You light up when you mention your family. Seamus, especially. I bet you're a lot like him."

"Light up? Uh-uh. Next you'll be saying I'm sweet and sentimental. I have a reputation to maintain, woman. I make a living being a tough guy." He gave her bottom a swat, then splayed his fingers there, massaging the spot as if the teasing tap might have stung. It hadn't. But there was something else on his mind. "You should think seriously about going back to school to become a doctor. I imagine I could use one."

Because he wanted her to stick around and be a part of his life for at least the six years it would take to complete her degrees? Instead of laughing at the self-deprecating joke as she was meant to, she shivered. There were no guarantees she'd have anything more than this night with Tom. Silas Danvers, Uncle Henry and a stash of illegal guns and blood money were waiting for them back at the compound. Tom had a job to do. He was already an hour into his night security shift. And though he'd called in on the walkie-talkie in his truck to say that he was on duty, eventually, they'd run into someone and he'd have to resume his Duff Maynard persona.

And she'd have to pretend that she didn't know about the guns or *Gin Rickey* or the way she longed for a new life with the real Detective Watson away from the farm.

"Hey." He tucked his fingers beneath her chin, turning her face up to his. "You doze off on me again? I fed you a great straight line I can't believe you're passing up."

Although her heart wasn't in it, she summoned a smart-aleck comeback about how no school in the world could teach her enough to keep him out of trouble. But before the words left her lips, Tom's entire body tensed beside her and his fingers moved up to cover her mouth.

Obeying the universal *shush* sign, Melanie reached for her clothes as Tom quickly tugged on his shorts and jeans, and pulled his gun from its holster. Now she could hear it, too—footsteps moving through the trees.

He motioned for her to stay down as he silently vaulted over the side of the truck and crept into the shadows.

She was dressed except for the zipper and flip-flops by the time she heard terse voices approaching.

"There was no call, no text. You know it's policy to get eyes on an operative when he misses a check-in."

She crouched in her hiding place until she recognized Tom's growly tone. "Something came up that needed to be dealt with. And turn those stupid flashlights off before somebody sees you."

Melanie peeked above the side of the truck to see Tom and two other men approaching. She recognized the blond MBI agent from the rainy night at the fire tower before their lights were quickly snuffed. Her eyes readjusted to the moonlight, but she still didn't recognize the second man, who wore a dark gray suit jacket and slacks, along with the gun strapped at his hip. Although he'd taken off his tie, he looked out of place in the casual world in which she lived. Another member of the task force?

As she scooted off the back of the pickup, Agent Benton eyed the rumpled blanket and her hastily dressed appearance. "Yeah, I see how you're dealing with it. This is how you handle someone blowing your cover?"

"Back off, Benton. Melanie's been an invaluable resource." Neither apologizing for nor explaining away what had just happened between them in the back of his truck, Tom swept her damp hair over the front of her shoulder and zipped up her dress. "I trust her to keep my identity and your operation a secret."

The dark-haired man she didn't know seemed vaguely familiar as he circled the truck, surveying the landscape, assessing the shadows. "You're sure, Duff? I remember Shayla Ortiz." When he got close enough for her to see his chiseled features above his open shirt collar, she realized he was a shorter, more polished version of Tom. He flashed her a smile as he extended his hand to her. "We haven't met yet. I'm Keir Watson."

"Watson?"

He held her hand as she tilted her questioning gaze up to Tom.

"Yep, he belongs to me." Tom smacked the younger man on the back of the head, urging him to release her. "Melanie Fiske, this is my brother, Keir. He's KCPD, too."

She remembered the tall, lanky doctor with the glasses. "How many brothers do you have?"

"Two. This pip-squeak is the youngest." Tom sat on the tailgate to pull on his socks and boots.

"And the handsomest. Nice to meet you." The *pip-squeak* looked fully grown, fully armed and completely dangerous despite his obvious charm. "This big doofus giving you any trouble? I'd be happy to rescue you."

"Really? Back off, little bro. You've already got a woman."

Keir answered with a soft laugh. "That I do. Kenna sends her regards."

"Regards?" Matt Benton swore under his breath. "I'll do a 360 to make sure there aren't eyes on us while you two share tea and crumpets. You Watsons have five minutes."

When the agent left to survey the surrounding

area, Keir propped his hands at his hips beneath his jacket. "Is Benton always this uptight?"

"Pretty much." Tom shrugged. "But he's good with paperwork and hoop jumping, so we make a good team. Everything all right at home? Grandpa? Dad?"

"They're good. Millie's worried that you're not eating enough. So not much has changed. Niall said you started the first day with a knife fight." He turned his startling blue eyes to Melanie. "Didn't know there was a woman in the picture, but then, Duff thinks grunts and curse words are the same thing as communication."

"Who's Shayla Ortiz?" Melanie asked, sinking onto the tailgate beside Tom, ignoring the innuendo in his brother's teasing.

"A mistake." He palmed the back of her neck and pulled her in for a quick, hard kiss. Melanie felt the responding heat creeping up her neck. "Go sit up in the cab of the truck. We won't be long. I need to chase these guys out of here before someone sees them." But Melanie was reluctant to move. There had to be a pressing reason for Tom's brother and handler to risk coming this far onto Fiske land. And that worried her. She could see Tom thinking about repeating the order, but he ended up shaking his head. "Or you could just stay here to get the task-force report and save me the trouble of repeating it." Soldier Tom with the clipped words and wary posture was back as he walked around to the gear box. He tossed his white shirt to Keir and pulled out a dark colored T-shirt to shrug into. "There's a sample of Silas Danvers's blood there. Benton will need it to confirm a match to the blood I found with the guns."

"Got it."

"If Benton says we've got five minutes, he'll be back in four and a half. So talk."

Despite the brotherly repartee they'd shared, Keir wasted no time telling him that Niall had done the autopsy on the body she'd found in Lake Hanover himself. "It's Richard Lloyd. Dental records match. Death by gunshot wound to the chest, close range. The lake was just the disposal site. Niall says he's been down there two months."

Tom paused in the middle of adjusting his shoulder holster across his back to squeeze Melanie's hand. Even though she'd halfway suspected the truth, they were talking about an old friend of hers, and the details weren't pretty. "Benton could have told me that. Why are you here?"

But Melanie wanted information, not sympathy. "Tom suspected there was a connection between Richard and your grandfather's shooting at your sister's wedding. Did you find evidence to support that?"

"Tom?" Keir seemed more surprised by the name than the fact she knew so many details about their family and Richard's death. But a glare from big brother sent Keir back into cop mode. "The coat he was wearing, his size and weight—he's a match for the guy who shot Grandpa. And that belt buckle you described is exactly what I saw on the guy. It's been identified in court records as belonging to a suspect involved with other shootings. Richard Lloyd is our hit man."

"Poor SueAnn." Melanie thought of her friend and how confirmation of her brother being murdered—of being a *murderer*—could worsen her precarious health. And then she wondered how Tom was handling this news. "I'm sorry the people I know had anything to do with hurting your family."

He responded with little more than a curt nod. The time for the emotional connection they'd shared tonight had passed. "We found cash confirming *Gin Rickey* is someone—or the code name for multiple someones—who lives here on the farm. Fiske or Danvers must have hired Lloyd out to do jobs."

"Any idea who hired him to come after us?" Keir asked.

Tom shook his head. "There might be something in the computer records I sent. They'll take a while to go through."

Melanie remembered her earlier encounter with Silas at the main house, when he'd worn the leather gloves. "Silas had a big envelope of some kind he handed to Henry. Could that have been a report—or record of whatever you're looking for?"

"Danvers doesn't strike me as someone who's into filing reports," Tom pointed out. "Did he say what was in the envelope?"

"Uncle Henry just called it 'the package,'" she answered. "Silas had been gone a long time. He could have driven into Falls City. Or even Kansas City.

Maybe there was cash in that envelope. I never saw inside it."

"All right, you two." Matt Benton reemerged from the trees. "Family fun time is over. The coast is clear for now, but can we get back to the business at hand?" He patted the pocket of his jacket. "I've got warrants. The judge thought those pictures you sent were enough to okay storming the compound and taking in Fiske, Danvers and anyone else with access to those guns. We'll seize the boats and vehicles, too, to let the CSIs go over them for trace evidence. The judge didn't want to wait and give them time to move the merchandise again."

Tom nodded. "I've confirmed they have multiple venues to bring the guns in and out of the area—"

"And multiple hiding places on the property," Melanie added. "There's a lot of acreage we haven't explored yet."

"We?" Agent Benton angled the brim of his ball cap and studied her as if he'd temporarily forgotten her existence. "Ma'am, if you've done anything to compromise this investigation—"

"You wouldn't have those warrants if it wasn't for her," Tom warned. He pocketed two spare magazines of bullets before closing the gear box. "What's our timeline look like?"

Agent Benton's threatening expression eased into simply unfriendly. "We're already blocking off the county highway and access roads, and any decent deputy is bound to report it. Apparently, Sheriff Cobb has been known to tip off Fiske whenever there's anything suspicious around the farm, so one of my men is keeping Cobb occupied in town going over the autopsy report. We'll be ready to move in sixty minutes."

Tom closed the tailgate and glanced down at Melanie before looking back at Keir and Benton. "Get her out of here. I don't want Mel anywhere near the raid. Make sure your men are well armed and wearing vests. I've already got Danvers on multiple counts of assault, and the key players are armed like a military unit. I have a feeling Fiske and his men won't go quietly. I'll go keep eyes on the compound to direct where to send in the troops."

They didn't have sixty minutes.

The walkie-talkie on Tom's front seat crackled with static. Instead of parting ways, the three men joined Melanie at the open driver's window to listen. The static cleared to the sound of a man's frantic voice. "Duff? Duff—it's Daryl. What's your twenty? Come back."

"They're looking for you." Keir's eyes narrowed with the same suspicion Tom's often did. "Could Cobb have already tipped them off?"

Agent Benton swore under his breath. "Could be a setup."

There was more static before the line cleared to some muttered reassurances. "Duff, this is Daryl. Is Mel with you? I need a medic."

Melanie opened the door and picked up the radio before anyone could stop her. She pressed the call button. "I'm here, Daryl. What's the problem? Over."

"Mel?" He exhaled an audible sigh of relief. "I'm at the infirmary with SueAnn. Her water broke. She's in labor."

"PUT HER IN my truck and let's go."

"Go where? Henry and Silas aren't going to let us drive off down the highway. If they don't stop us, they'll at least follow us to make sure we're going to the hospital, and then they'll see your roadblock. She certainly can't hike out through the hills in her condition." Melanie unwrapped the blood-pressure cuff and jotted down SueAnn's vitals. They weren't good. The baby's heartbeat was strong, but if SueAnn couldn't start recovering her own pulse and heart rate between contractions, there was no way she'd be able to deliver the baby vaginally before they both suffered irreparable damage or died.

She felt a firm hand on her shoulder and looked up into Tom's stony expression. "Doc, we can't stay. My team is en route. I can't guarantee anyone's safety here."

SueAnn had collapsed against the pillow and closed her eyes. Daryl turned to Melanie. "It's not good, is it?"

She knew he was referring to his wife's condition, not Tom's cryptic warning. She wasn't even sure Daryl had realized how well armed the man standing over them was, or if he understood the covert warnings about the imminent danger. Melanie shook her head. "She's not strong enough to deliver the baby here. She needs a real doctor."

Daryl pushed to his feet. "Screw Henry and his rules. Tell me what to do to get one here. I've already lost my best friend. I'm not going to lose her and my son or daughter."

"We're not bringing anyone else onto this compound." Tom pushed aside the eyelet curtains and scanned outside, his body on full alert. "The dance is breaking up. People are on the move."

She crossed to him and rested a hand on his arm, willing him to look at her. "Tom."

He glanced down into her eyes and shook his head. "That's not fair, babe."

"There's another way off this farm."

He shook his head again, understanding what she was asking. "Can she make that trek?"

"*We* can."

"Get her prepped." He pulled out his cell and punched in a number. "Keir. I've got an emergency medical evac. A woman's in labor and she's having complications. We'll bring her to your location at the fire tower. Have an ambulance meet us there."

Like Tom, Melanie moved into action. There might be bullets flying soon. There would certainly be chaos once a team of law-enforcement agents arrived. With roads closing, the help SueAnn needed might not get here in time if they waited. Risking a jarring ride had to be better than the nothing she could do here. She stood beside Daryl and pointed to the corners of the blanket where SueAnn lay. "We'll use this as a makeshift stretcher and carry her."

"Let me do that." Tom nudged her aside and

pushed the phone into her hands. "Give Keir whatever medical info he needs and he'll relay it to the paramedics." There was a nagging little memory dancing at the corner of her mind when she took the phone, but there was no time to make sense of it before Tom ordered her to move. "My truck leaves in sixty seconds."

While Tom and Daryl carried SueAnn out the front door, she stuffed SueAnn's file into her paramedic's backpack, grabbed an extra blanket and pillow and hurried outside, giving Keir an approximate ETA before ending the call. Earlier, she'd spared a few precious minutes to change into her jeans and hiking boots, so it was easy for her to hop into the bed of the truck beside her patient. She tapped the roof of the truck cab, indicating they were as ready as they were going to get, and Tom shifted into gear. He kept his headlights off for as long as possible before the gravel road reached the tree line to mask their escape. Encouraging Daryl to talk in soothing tones to keep SueAnn as calm as possible, she stuffed the pillow under SueAnn's knees and covered her with the warm blanket.

"I guess we kind of broke up the dance." Daryl held tightly to his wife's hand. "Abby said I should take her straight to the infirmary. Folks were askin' where you and Duff had got off to. I tried callin' your phone, but there was no answer. Lots of folks tried. You're gonna have a bunch of messages when you check your voice mail." He sort of laughed, though it sounded more like a squashed-up sob. "Silas was the one who said he saw you headin' off to the lake with Duff."

"Silas saw us?" So much for shaming him into silence.

"Yeah. That's why I called you on the radio."

"Where's Silas now?"

Daryl shrugged. "Last I knew, Abby was brewin' him a pot of coffee at the main house to sober him up. He was pretty pissed that Deanna snuck out of the dance with Roy before it was over."

That wasn't why he was pissed.

"How many people called my phone?" Melanie's stomach sank as they bounced over the next rut.

"I don't know. Five or six. Maybe more."

She hadn't gotten any of those messages because she'd left her phone in Henry and Abby's attic.

MELANIE HEARD THE rumble of ATV motors cutting through the sticky night air as soon as Tom skidded to a stop on the muddy gravel near the *Edwina*.

"Why did you tell me to stop?" Tom hurried around the truck. From the angle of his gaze, she knew he'd heard the ATVs approaching, too. "Is SueAnn all right?"

"This is my fault. I'm so sorry." Melanie jumped out of the truck bed as soon as Tom lowered the tailgate. She pointed to the distant engine noises echoing throughout the hills. "We only have a couple of minutes before they'll be here."

"Sorry about what? We need to keep moving."

"Silas might not have reported seeing you and me

in the main house. But a ringing telephone would certainly have sent someone upstairs to look." She pulled out the pocket linings of her jeans to show him the problem. "I left my phone in the attic. Everyone's been calling me. They'll know we were there. Even if they don't figure out you're a cop, they'll know you're a traitor. They'll know *I'm* a traitor."

Instead of placing blame, Tom grasped her on either side of her waist and lifted her back into the truck. "They're probably moving the guns right now."

"Or following us." She jumped back to the ground and Tom cursed. "With those small vehicles, they're going to be more maneuverable on the terrain between here and the fire tower, and they'll catch us in no time. We need to split up."

"No. When Silas and whoever's with him get here, it's not going to be an argument. They eliminate people who know their secret and won't keep it. Get in the damn truck."

When he reached for her again, she twisted out of his grasp. "You know I'm right. You need to get to a spot where you can notify your team to move in now, before all the evidence is gone. And I sure don't want SueAnn in the line of fire if they catch us."

The engines were getting louder.

"I don't want anyone in the line of fire. This is my job, Melanie. This isn't your fight."

"The hell it isn't." She held out her hand, hearing the noise of the approaching ATVs like grasping hands clawing over her skin. "Give me the keys to your truck. I can lead them away from the fire tower and your friends. They won't expect you to be on foot, and the two of you can make better time than if I'm carrying her."

He pulled his keys from his pocket, but held them tight in his fist. "You go to the rendezvous. Keir will be there to meet you. I'll play decoy."

"No. Get SueAnn out of here. It takes two people to handle that stretcher and I can't carry her that far. Not fast enough."

"Doc—"

She snatched the keys from his hand and dashed to the front of the truck. "Stop arguing with me! Save her. Get the bad guys. You promised."

Tom was there at the door when she started the engine. "I'll keep that promise. *Everything* I promised." He pulled something else from his pocket and handed it to her through the open window. It was her father's pocket watch. "Your good luck charm."

"Thanks." She stuffed it into her pocket. "You're not going to arrest me for driving without a license, are you?" When he didn't laugh, she turned away to start the engine. She couldn't look at that tight clench of his jaw and know how much he wanted to save her. "I'll be fine. I'll ditch the truck somewhere and hide until they're gone. I've been hiding in these hills for years now."

His big hand reached through the open window to palm the back of her neck. He kissed her, all that emotion on his face branding her with a hard, possessive stamp on her lips. She touched her fingers to his jaw, answering back with the same raw promise before he broke away. "I'm coming back for you. You are not alone in this fight." He caught a lock of her hair between his fingers as he stepped back. "I'll be back for you."

"Tom…"

He squeezed his eyes shut and shook his head as if he didn't want to hear his real name. Then those green eyes popped open. "I love you."

She summoned a croaky whisper that was a stunned mixture of joy, fear and piss-poor timing. "I love you, too."

But Tom and Daryl were already at the back of the truck, lifting SueAnn on the homemade stretcher. He slammed the tailgate as if he'd spanked her bottom, spurring her into action. "Go!"

With the two men moving in a quick march, hauling SueAnn on the blanket between them, Melanie stomped on the accelerator. The truck fishtailed, spitting up twigs and mud until the tires found traction and she sped off around the lake.

FORTY MINUTES LATER, Melanie's thighs ached from maintaining her crouched position up on a wide limb of an ancient pin oak where she'd often come to read as a little girl. The noise of the ATV engines had stopped, and the crackle of walkie-talkie static and men's voices had faded into the distance. Since she hadn't heard any mention of Duff Maynard or Sergeant Loser or some other stupid nickname referring to Tom on the radio, she prayed that meant he'd gotten SueAnn to his brother and a waiting ambulance.

She perched in her hiding spot until the only noise she could hear was the breeze moving through the leaves. Hoping it was safe to make her way back to the fire tower and let Tom know he didn't have to worry about her, she climbed down. It would be a long hike, but she still had a couple of hours of night sky and shadows to hide in before the sun came up. That should give her plenty of time to skirt the compound and avoid company before she ran into the backup Tom had promised.

She hoped Tom was safe. She hoped he loved her enough to take her home to Kansas City to meet the rest of his family. And though in some ways it felt as though she'd be leaving her father behind her, she hoped with every cell of her being that she never had to come back to this beautiful prison of a life.

She allowed herself to finally inhale a deep breath.

And then she heard the unmistakable sound of a gun being cocked behind her. Melanie stopped at the harsh metallic rasp, her hopes washing away with the lake beside her. She slipped her fingers into her pocket to touch her father's watch, reminding herself she wasn't alone.

Henry Fiske was smiling when she turned to face the barrel of his gun. "You've always been trouble, haven't you, girl?"

Chapter Fifteen

Melanie wondered if her father had taken a similar boat ride on board the *Edwina* the night he'd died.

Her uncle steered the *August Moon* over waves that got choppy as they neared the dam. Boating at night without any lights was dangerous, but as she swayed on her seat above the fishing deck, she knew safety wasn't Henry's concern.

She'd forgotten her uncle had grown up in these hills, just like she had. She should have stayed hidden longer. But she had a feeling it would have only been a matter of time before Henry tracked her down and made her pay for her defiance. One thing she hadn't forgotten about her uncle was how much he hated anyone who didn't follow his rules and blindly go along with his plans. But she was past the point of pretending she didn't hate him and what he'd done to control her life. She was only glad that Tom wasn't here, that he'd gotten away, that he would live to destroy the three people on the boat with her.

The two-way radio in the cockpit flared to life with static and the sound of Roy Cassmeyer's voice.

"Mr. Fiske? This is Roy. Do you read me? Over." There were a few more seconds of static. "Sir? We've got a situation at the compound. What should I—?"

"Turn that thing off," Abby groused from her seat across from Melanie.

Henry severed the connection and shut off the radio.

Tom and his task force must be the *situation* Roy was dealing with.

Silas jerked the rope he was tying around her wrists. "What are you smilin' about?"

She wouldn't give him the satisfaction of yelping at the pinch of pain. She wouldn't argue against the gun her aunt trained on her while Silas tossed two of the heavy bags of guns overboard. They floated on the surface for a few seconds, but started sinking before the boat left them in its silvery wake and they disappeared into the darkness. That's what was in store for her, too. "Did you kill my father like this?"

Abby reached into a third bag at her feet. "You don't know when to let a thing drop, do you? You're just as stubborn as Leroy was. He wouldn't do what he was told, either." She pulled out Melanie's cell phone and waved it in front of her before tossing it overboard. Melanie heard a splash, but couldn't see much beyond the *Moon*'s shiny white bulwarks. "You went snooping again. And I asked you not to." She kicked the heavy bag toward Silas and ordered him to tie it to Melanie's waist. "Now I have to throw all this merchandise away. Our buyers will be disappointed. But it's better than being put out of business."

If only she knew.

Silas's bruised face hovered in front of her. There was no pretense of politeness when he dragged her to her feet and looped a length of rope behind her, pulling her against him. "Where is your boyfriend? Is he a cop? How long have you been helping him spy on us? We're gonna kill him, too, you know."

"Take your filthy hands off me." Bound, but not defenseless, Melanie sank her teeth into his arm. With a bellowing curse, he drew back to strike her. But she rammed her shoulder into his gut, knocking him off balance. They crashed into the side railing, rocking the boat when they hit. Water splashed over the side, soaking the front of his shirt.

Seeing Silas's stunned look, she thought she'd found her chance to escape. She pulled herself up to the railing. Swimming would be difficult with her limbs tied, but impossible once they tied the heavy weight of the gun bag to her body.

A hard, cold piece of steel pressed into the back of her skull, stopping her. "Sit."

Obeying Abby's gun, Melanie crawled to the stern, finding a place to sit more easily than Silas was finding a way to stand again. While a part of her reveled in his discomfort and the knowledge they hadn't found Tom yet, another part still wanted answers. She looked beyond her aunt and the white-knuckled Silas to Henry. "You said you loved your brother. Did you kill him? Is that why talking about him upsets you?"

Abby sat, keeping the gun trained on her. "*I* killed

your father. We wanted to include him in our plans to turn this place into a gold mine. But he was all about living off the land and not wanting anything dangerous to happen around his little girl. We had our own daughter to provide for, and I wasn't about to raise Deanna as some poor, backwater hillbilly." Melanie thought that simple life had been pretty special. "How did Leroy think we were going to get the money to transform this place into what it's become? Selling a few doughnuts and handmade tables? We offered to buy his half, but he refused. When he threatened to report us for having such forward-thinking ideas, he and Henry got into a fight. I had to save my husband's life. I hit him with this very gun." She leaned back, perhaps thinking Melanie would turn submissive with shock or grief and shut up. "With the storm that night, it was easy enough to stage an accident with the *Edwina*."

Coldhearted bitch. For a few seconds, Melanie wondered how well her aunt could swim. "Why spare me? Once I was old enough to understand such things, I could have contested your claim to the land."

"Couldn't kill a child. And why make a fuss? You were happy with us, weren't you?" Until she wasn't anymore. That's why they'd tightened their control of her life. No wonder they'd pressured her to find a man and stay on the farm.

"Your guns kill children." She was beyond feeling pain or regret. "You hired Richard out to kill people. That's what all those disposable phones in the attic were for. Call *Gin Rickey* if you need a job done. Did you kill him, too?"

"Richard got himself into trouble all on his own. When the last client who hired him wasn't satisfied, we agreed to help dispose of the body to assure customer satisfaction, and so he couldn't be traced back to us. We like our privacy here."

"You weren't expecting Roy to snag him with the propeller, were you?" She imagined that discovery had set a whole lot of scrambling to save the family business into motion. "Who hired him?"

"A lot of people. They didn't volunteer the information. Once they paid the fee, I wasn't all that interested in exchanging names."

Silas stumbled to her seat at the back of the boat. He secured her ankles to the bags that would drag her to the bottom of the lake. But Melanie had one last question she needed answered first. "Did any of them hire Richard to shoot up a wedding at a church in Kansas City?"

"Always so many questions. It really is quite tedious, dear. Not a trait that men like."

Henry finally joined the conversation. "I know I'm bored with it." He stopped the engine and let the boat glide to a stop. "We should be in deep-enough water here. Even if you did call the cops on us, girl, they won't find anything. No guns. No witness."

"I guess you're going to die an old maid, after all." Abby nodded to Silas.

Still looking a little queasy, he picked up Melanie and set her on the aft fishing deck.

Once her aunt stopped talking, Melanie heard a different sound. The growl of an engine. Something much bigger than any ATV.

Hope surged through her. She wasn't alone, after all.

"Now!" Henry ordered. "We need to clear this boat."

Silas set the bags on the deck beside her. But when Melanie refused to take that fatal step herself, he pulled his knife. When he thrust it at her, she grabbed his belt and pulled him into the water with her.

Blood filled the water around her as Silas dragged her down into the darkness.

DUFF LOOKED AT the infant sleeping in a blue knit cap in the Saint Luke's Hospital nursery, hoping the fatigue, fear and coffee churning in his stomach didn't reach his face and scare the kid. Or the grandparents sliding him wary looks. Or the nurse he'd snapped at when she'd asked him to return to the surgical ICU waiting area. He'd already worn a path in the carpet there, waiting to hear if Melanie would be downgraded from critical to stable condition after surgery to repair the lung Silas Danvers had cut open, trying to save himself from drowning. He barely remembered the one-sided firefight between Matt Benton and the Fiskes before they'd surrendered and he'd dived into the lake to save her.

He nodded his acquiescence when a woman in pink scrubs approached him. "I know. I'll leave."

Duff replayed the words the medics had told him

when he'd finally gotten Melanie on a boat and mede-vaced her on a helicopter waiting at the Fiske compound. There were worries about infection from the lake water that had gotten inside her body, layers of muscle and skin to repair. A whole lot of blood loss.

He got on the elevator and rode down to the second floor, remembering other things, too. Melanie had talked a lot at first when he'd pulled her on board the *Ozark Dreamer*. She'd tried to tell him how to stanch the wound, how to relieve the pressure around her collapsed lung. She'd told him what she'd learned from Henry and Abby, despite him telling her to shut up and save her strength. But then she'd stopped talking. His love and his prayers hadn't been enough to keep her with him.

Keir had driven him to Saint Luke's while Mel was in surgery. His dad had brought him a change of clothes. Sleep wasn't really an option until he knew Melanie was going to wake up and talk to him again.

The elevator opened to the sound of a squealing baby, and for a split second, he wondered if he'd remembered to push the elevator button. But then he saw the plump, silver-haired woman holding the happy infant, Duff's future nephew, as an eighty-year-old retired cop, standing with the aid of a walker, tickled the infant's tummy.

"Grandpa."

Seamus greeted him with a slurred tone of concern. "Son. How ah you?"

"How are you, old man?" he tried to tease.

"Ah'll hang in there if you will."

Millie Leighter's blue eyes were shiny with tears when she tipped her face up for Duff to kiss her cheek. "We're so worried about you. We're keeping you and Melanie in our prayers."

"Thanks. Any news?"

She shook her head before pressing her cheek to Seamus's shoulder. Seamus patted her arm in comfort. Millie might not be blood, but she was definitely family.

Stopping at the coffee machine to consider another cup, Duff was greeted by Niall's fiancée, Lucy McKane. The petite brunette slipped her arms around his waist and squeezed him in a hug. Her eyes were a little misty, too, when she pulled away. "We're all anxious to meet Melanie. I know we're going to love her as much as you do." She held up the baby bottle in her hand. "I'd better go feed Tommy."

He shouldn't have been surprised to see the rest of his family when he entered the waiting room. Keir and his fiancée, Kenna Parker, were there, sharing a conversation with his grandfather's nurse, Jane Boyle. His sister, Liv, jumped up from her chair and dashed across the room to give him a hug, followed more slowly by her husband, Gabe Knight, with a handshake.

"You know they have the best doctors here," Gabe offered.

"I know."

Liv brushed her short brown bangs off her forehead. "Niall went to the front desk to see if he could talk to the doctor who performed the surgery and give us a report." She squeezed his arm. "Maybe you should try to get some rest?"

With a noncommittal nod, Duff walked on past them to the man he was proud to be a carbon copy of in so many ways. Green eyes, brown hair, stocky build, a badge. He sank into the chair beside his father. Thomas Watson Sr. was a solid, steady presence who thankfully didn't ask him how he was feeling or offer any platitudes. Thomas put his hand on Duff's shoulder and simply sat in silence with him for several minutes.

While he had no doubt of his family's love and support, Duff couldn't help but remember a similar gathering the night his mother had died. They'd rushed her to the hospital, but she'd never had a chance. Duff braced his elbows on his knees and leaned forward. "How did you do it, Dad? How did you survive when the woman you love is… And you can't save her…and…?"

Thomas squeezed his shoulder and nodded to the rest of the room. "I had my family."

Niall strode into the room, with Seamus and Millie and all the others gathering behind him as he crossed to Duff. "Melanie's awake. She came through surgery just fine. She'll be sore for a while, but she's breathing on her own. They've moved her to a private room. You can go see her."

Duff was already on his way.

His only hesitation came when he first pushed open the door and saw her lying on the hospital bed. With beeping machines, and tubes and needles hooked into her arm, this was a much more modern version of the infirmary she'd built back in her cottage. Tears stung his eyes. She looked so pale except for her rich, beautiful hair, fanned across the pillow like an auburn halo. He was supposed to be so damn tough, the man who could handle whatever was necessary to get a job done. But he was about to stand here and cry like a baby until Melanie blinked her eyes open and smiled.

"I finally made it to Kansas City."

Tom laughed and hurried to her side. He leaned over to kiss her lightly on the forehead, not wanting to do anything that might hurt her. He pulled up a stool to sit as close to her as he dared and captured her hand in both of his. He nodded to the big basket that had been delivered to the table on the opposite side of the bed. "I didn't know what kind of flowers you like, so I got you books. Bought a copy of everything they had down in the hospital gift shop."

Turning her head, she reached over with her taped-up hand to finger the spine of one of the paperbacks. "I love them. I'm going to need a new bookshelf."

"I'll get you one. Whatever it takes to convince you to stay with me."

"To stay...?" He didn't have an engagement ring, but he reached into his pocket for something he thought she'd like better. He pressed her father's watch into her hand. She carried it to her lips before setting it beside her and linking her fingers with his again. "Thank you."

"That was smart to leave it at the boat dock so I

knew where to find you. Your dad would have been proud of you."

"Sorry I couldn't find out who hired Richard to shoot your grandfather."

"We'll get him. We're a lot closer to the truth now, thanks to you." He brushed aside a lock of hair that wasn't really out of place. "In the meantime, I'll settle for getting a lot of illegal guns off the street and making my city a little bit safer."

"Silas?"

"Dead. He ran into his knife multiple times. I helped him." He recalled the short fight in the lake vividly. Stopping Danvers for good had been the only way he could get past him to reach Melanie and pull her to safety.

"Henry and Abby?"

"Arrested. Along with Roy, Sterling Cobb and a few others."

"SueAnn?"

Tom grinned. "Boy. Daryl Jr. The doctor delivered him by C-section, so they're staying here a few days longer for observation. But they're both going to be fine."

"You? You look tired."

"Nothing seeing your pretty brown eyes can't fix."

He leaned in to kiss her again, but the door swung open and a parade of well-wishers filed in. Watsons, soon-to-be Watsons, four generations of Watsons— bringing flowers, sharing embarrassing stories about how Tom was on a first-name basis with the ER doctors at Saint Luke's, thanking her for helping with his investigation, inviting her to dinner, inviting her to Niall and Lucy's wedding, wishing her well.

Then, in a flurry of waves and handshakes, Jane Boyle donned her nurse persona, said Melanie needed her rest and shooed them out. The room seemed conspicuously quiet after they'd gone, but his father was right—they'd left a lot of love and support in their wake.

"As you can see, you probably won't ever be alone again if you hang out with me here in KC."

Melanie was smiling right along with him. "Did you mean what you said before? I can stay with you?"

"Didn't I prove I was a man of my word?"

"I never should have doubted you."

"Well, I did lie to you. In the beginning."

"And I was headstrong and independent and refused to use your nickname. I don't know why you ever picked me to help with your mission."

"I picked you because you were headstrong and independent and refused to use my nickname." Tom paused and grinned. "And the red hair." He caught a silky lock between his fingers. "Love the red hair."

Melanie laughed. She instantly grabbed her stomach and grimaced. "That hurts."

Tom shot to his feet. "I'll get a nurse."

She grabbed his hand, stopping him. "I love you, Tom."

He lowered his hip to the edge of her bed. "I love you."

She stroked her fingers across his jaw before cupping his cheek. He knew he needed a shave, but she was smiling. "I like this look even better than date-night Tom."

"What does that mean?"

"I'll explain later. After you kiss me. Lips this time. Like you mean it."

He did.

Epilogue

The unhappy man watched one Watson after another file out of the redhead's hospital room. They were happy, chatting excitedly, sharing relief, making plans.

He'd had a plan, too. One that each of those Watson boys had screwed up in one way or another. He knew they'd suffered. He'd *made* them suffer. And still they hugged and laughed, held hands and smiled. It wasn't fair. The woman he loved couldn't laugh or smile anymore. He couldn't hold her ever again, and it was their fault. It was Thomas Watson's fault.

He waited for them to gather their things and get on the elevator—two elevators since there were so many of them. His pool of contracted help had vanished with the dustup at the Fiske Farm. There was no *Gin Rickey* for him to call anymore. Not that that moron had been able to complete the job the way he'd wanted. He would have to take care of business himself.

While the second group of Watsons waited for the next elevator, he watched the pretty nurse in the blue scrubs separate herself from the others to pull her cell phone from her pocket. She'd been living with them for months now, taking care of the old man, bossing everybody around. He didn't think they liked her much, judging by the arguments that seemed to flare up when she was around, but she must be good at her job if they were keeping her...

Hold on. The woman pressed her hand against her forehead, the conversational tone of her call changing to heated whispers.

And then he saw Thomas's reaction to her distress. That stolen look of concern. That deep breath before he left the group at the elevator to join her.

The man watching would have laughed if he'd been willing to reveal his presence.

Watson was making this too easy. The big papa bear had the hots for the live-in nurse. As he watched Thomas walk over to comfort Ms. Boyle, he knew there was an even better way to make Detective Lieutenant Thomas Watson Sr. pay for his crime. His efforts to destroy the Watson family hadn't worked. But he could still make Thomas pay.

He could hurt the woman he loved...

* * * * *

COMING NEXT MONTH FROM
⊕ HARLEQUIN®
™

INTRIGUE

Available May 23, 2017

YOU CAN FIND MORE INFORMATION ON UPCOMING HARLEQUIN® TITLES, FREE EXCERPTS AND MORE AT WWW.HARLEQUIN.COM.

HICNM0517

He knew he had to utilize her somehow, and maybe
she could be useful. "All right, you might as well come
along. You might come in handy if there's a next of kin
to notify." Ronan began walking back to his car. "I'm not
much good at that."

"I'm surprised," Sierra commented.

Reaching the car, Ronan turned to look at her. "If
you're going to be sarcastic—"

"No, I'm serious," she told him, then went on to
explain her rationale. "You're so detached, I just assumed
it wouldn't bother you to tell a person that someone
they'd expected to come home was never going to do that
again. It would bother them, of course," she couldn't help
adding, "but not you."

Ronan got into his vehicle, buckled up and pulled
out in what seemed like one fluid motion, all the while

chewing on what this latest addition to his team had just said. Part of him just wanted to let it go. But he couldn't.

"I'm not heartless," he informed her. "I just don't allow emotions to get in the way and I don't believe in using more words than are absolutely necessary," he added pointedly since he knew that seemed to bother her.

"Well, lucky for you, I do," she told him with what amounted to the beginnings of a smile. "I guess that's what'll make us such good partners."

He looked at her, stunned. He viewed them as being like oil and water—never able to mix. "Is that your take on this?" he asked incredulously.

"Yes," she answered cheerfully.

The fact that she appeared to have what one of his brothers would label a "killer smile" notwithstanding, Ronan just shook his head. "Unbelievable."

"Oh, you'll get to believe it soon enough," she told him. Before he could say anything, Sierra just continued talking to him and got down to the immediate business at hand. "I'm going to need to see your files on the other murders once we're back in the squad room so I can be brought up to date."

He didn't even spare her a look. "Fine."

"Are you always this cheerful?" she asked. "Or is there something in particular that's bothering you?"

Don't miss
CAVANAUGH STANDOFF by Marie Ferrarella,
available June 2017 wherever
Harlequin® Intrigue books and ebooks are sold.

www.Harlequin.com

Get 2 Free Books,
Plus 2 Free Gifts—
just for trying the Reader Service!

HARLEQUIN

INTRIGUE

YES! Please send me 2 FREE Harlequin® Intrigue novels and my 2 FREE gifts (gifts are worth about $10 retail). After receiving them, if I don't wish to receive any more books, I can return the shipping statement marked "cancel." If I don't cancel, I will receive 6 brand-new novels every month and be billed just $4.99 each for the regular-print edition or $5.74 each for the larger-print edition in the U.S., or $5.74 each for the regular-print edition or $6.49 each for the larger-print edition in Canada. That's a savings of at least 12% off the cover price! It's quite a bargain! Shipping and handling is just 50¢ per book in the U.S. and 75¢ per book in Canada.* I understand that accepting the 2 free books and gifts places me under no obligation to buy anything. I can always return a shipment and cancel at any time. Even if I never buy another book, the two free books and gifts are mine to keep forever.

Please check one: ☐ Harlequin® Intrigue Regular-Print ☐ Harlequin® Intrigue Larger-Print
(182/382 HDN GLP2)   (199/399 HDN GLP3)

Name _____ (PLEASE PRINT) _____

Address _____ Apt. # _____

City _____ State/Prov. _____ Zip/Postal Code _____

Signature (if under 18, a parent or guardian must sign) _____

Mail to the **Reader Service:**
IN U.S.A.: P.O. Box 1867, Buffalo, NY 14240-1867
IN CANADA: P.O. Box 611, Fort Erie, Ontario L2A 9Z9

*Terms and prices subject to change without notice. Prices do not include applicable taxes. Sales tax applicable in N.Y. Canadian residents will be charged applicable taxes. Offer not valid in Quebec. This offer is limited to one order per household. Books received may not be as shown. Not valid for current subscribers to Harlequin Intrigue books. All orders subject to credit approval. Credit or debit balances in a customer's account(s) may be offset by any other outstanding balance owed by or to the customer. Please allow 4 to 6 weeks for delivery. Offer available while quantities last.

Your Privacy—The Reader Service is committed to protecting your privacy. Our Privacy Policy is available online at www.ReaderService.com or upon request from the Reader Service.

We make a portion of our mailing list available to reputable third parties that offer products we believe may interest you. If you prefer that we not exchange your name with third parties, or if you wish to clarify or modify your communication preferences, please visit us at www.ReaderService.com/consumerschoice or write to us at Reader Service Preference Service, P.O. Box 9062, Buffalo, NY 14240-9062. Include your complete name and address.

HI17

Love the Harlequin book you just read?

Your opinion matters.

Review this book on your favorite book site, review site, blog or your own social media properties and share your opinion with other readers!